MYTH MISTRESS & THE BO PEEP KILLER

Mark Turner

dizzyemupublishing.com

DIZZY EMU PUBLISHING

1714 N McCadden Place, Hollywood, Los Angeles 90028

dizzyemupublishing.com

Myth Mistress & The Bo Peep Killer
Mark Turner

First published in the United States
in 2022 by Dizzy Emu Publishing

dizzyemupublishing.com

MYTH MISTRESS & THE BO PEEP KILLER

Mark Turner

Myth Mistress & The Bo Peep Killer

Written

by

Mark Turner

themarkturner@gmail.com

FADE IN:

COMPUTER SCREEN

A welcome video plays full screen. A beautiful college
student, MYTH MISTRESS, speaks into the camera.

                    MYTH MISTRESS
               (phony excitement)
          You want to know if the latest internet
          rumors are true or not? Are you in
          search of facts to prove your idiot
          roommate wrong? Do you want to know if
          Elvis is still alive? Well, then...
               (nasty)
          This site is NOT for you, you dim-witted
          nimrods! All you dopes go to "Snopes!"
          You're not smart enough to be here! Get
          the F off my site!
               (back to normal)
          This is Myth Mistress dot com, the
          internet's go-to source for total
          immersion into urban myths and legends!
          MUFON's got nothing on us! Except,
          they've been around longer!

The video stops.

INT. MYTH BUNKER - NIGHT

A computer geek's dream dorm room - three large monitors,
cameras mounted front, behind, and in the corner of the
ceiling for a full room view - all streaming live through her
website, MYTHMISTRESS.COM.

Myth Mistress, dressed in a skin-tight black rubber
dominatrix outfit sans long rubber gloves and mask, walks the
"catwalk" turning and posing like a supermodel before heading
to the controls.

                    MYTH MISTRESS
          I'm your lovely Mistress of Myth, a
          curator of legends, sexy enough to raise
          the dead! Or raise something... if you
          get my drift. Welcome to my Myth Bunker.

Live comments stream on one monitor.

**U R SO HOT! I LOVE U MYTH MISTRESS! U R MINE! NO SHE'S
MINE. I WANT US TO BE TOGETHER. FOREVER! YOWZA! I WANT TO
BE YOU! WOMEN LOVE MYTHS 2!**

Comments stream by with "likes" and "hearts" flowing by.

                    MYTH MISTRESS
          Here at Myth Mistress dot com, we don't
          deal in fact or fiction, our *raison
          d'etre* are things that go bump in the
          night... ghosts, demons, UFOS, or the
          Missouri Mo Mo.
                (beat)
          We are true believers, but not gullible
          morons, like my roommate, Milly! We WANT
          to believe! But we're more Fox Mulders
          with Dana Scully brains! If a myth or
          legend exists we want to know about it.
          Any myth. Every legend... old, or new,
          we want to know when, where, how, and why
          it started, is it real, could it be real,
          and so on... THAT'S what we're all about!
                (beat)
          We say, "Wouldn't it be sick to discover
          vampires are real?!" A bloodthirsty
          creature that DOESN'T sparkle like a
          fucking cunt and brood over depressed
          Goth chicks. The ones that turn into
          bats, suck your blood and sleep in
          coffins. WE think THAT would be dope!

She strolls over to pick up her long rubber gloves and
begins, slowly, seductively, pulling them on.

                    MYTH MISTRESS (cont'd)
          We'd love to discover alligators living
          in New York sewers! It makes sense. But
          is it true? Probably not in New York,
          but Florida, or Louisiana... who knows?
          That's why our motto is quaerite et
          vincas! Seek and destroy!
                (beat)
          Is little red riding hood simply a story
          told in the middle ages because a wolf
          ate a grandmother to trick a little girl
          into giving up her goodies? Hell, no!
          It was a cautionary tale that served a
          purpose.

A comment pops up on her screen from Mythmama14.

TO KEEP KIDS OUT OF THE WOODS!

                    MYTH MISTRESS
          That's right, Mythmama14! And I'd say
          it's a warning not to let men trick them
          into giving up their goodies, as well!
          So, it still works today.
                (beat)
          Hey, speaking of Red Riding Hood, it's
          Halloween!

                    MYTH MISTRESS (CONT'D)
          And tonight is our third Halloween live
          streaming event! So, thanks for
          watching...

She looks at the viewer count in the corner of the website.

                    MYTH MISTRESS (cont'd)
          ... all two hundred of you? C'mon, guys,
          we have ten thousand subscribers! I know
          it's early, but this is a huge event. We
          need it to be a great show! I got
          sponsors involved this year!
                    (beat)
          Yeah, as in, FREE Bud Light at Kappa
          Alpha Psi, and Sig Chi parties! All
          because of Myth Mistress dot com. So
          c'mon! Let's go! Call your friends.
                    (beat)
          We need millions to tune in to get the
          sponsors to do this again! All you
          campus subscribers come find me! We'll
          have a beer together. But stay tuned in
          on your phone! It's way more fun that
          way! Here... retweet this...

She grabs her phone, talking as she types.

                    MYTH MISTRESS (cont'd)
          Be sure to tune into my Halloween live
          stream event... Or else!
                    (beat)
          You'll miss all the member videos and my
          live stream from all the campus Halloween
          parties throughout the night.

COMPUTER SCREEN

Words scroll across the screen: BE SURE TO STAY GLUED TO MY
HALLOWEEN LIVE STREAM EVENT... Or else!

MYTH BUNKER

                    MYTH MISTRESS
          There! It's in the tweetersphere.
          Subscribers do your thing. People on
          campus tweet out the link to your friends
          and enemies. Come get your party on!
          Don't cost nothing!

A somewhat awkward, plain-looking, twenty-year-old woman,
MILLY, walks into the myth bunker. She's one of those orange-
haired gingers with freckles and a constant look of surprise
on her face.

Looking down at her phone as she enters.

                    MILLY
          Kim! I told you to take me off your
          stupid tweeter blasts!

She looks up realizing she's being broadcast.

                    MYTH MISTRESS
          Damn it, Milly, I told you NOT to walk
          into the myth bunker unless you're
          invited! You're never invited, by the
          way! So, bounce betty, make tracks back
          to that house of horrors you call a room!

                    MILLY
          Fuck you, bitch! The last thing I want
          is to be on your stupid show. You act
          like you're all intellectual, but you're
          just a slut prancing around like a porn
          star.

                    MYTH MISTRESS
          Don't hate cause you can't participate.
          Jealous is an ugly color on you, Milly.
          It clashes with that orange hair.
               (to the front camera)
          Hey, guys, muddle-headed Milly's lack of
          self-awareness is so well documented that
          she's become an urban legend herself!
          Watch this.

Myth Mistress clicks on a video.

COMPUTER SCREEN

Full-screen video cuts of Milly walking around looking
confused, picking her nose while reading, coming out of the
bathroom with toilet paper hanging out of her pants, walking
into a wall while texting, over-startled screaming when
someone knocks on the door, walking and farting with each
step, and it continues, as we return to...

MYTH BUNKER

                    MILLY
          You're gonna pay for embarrassing me with
          that video!

                    MYTH MISTRESS
          Milly, Milly, Milly, you embarrass
          yourself. I just record it, edit it, and
          play it all the time for others to enjoy.

                    MILLY
          You cow! You're just a rubber wrapped
          slut!

                    MYTH MISTRESS
          Once again you are wrong, Mildred, while
          I do like the way rubber feels on my
          skin... I am not a slut.

Myth Mistress marches toward Milly.

                    MYTH MISTRESS (cont'd)
          I am a strong feminine woman who is
          attractive, uses her sexuality wisely,
          and likes to dress seductively by wearing
          skintight rubber outfits, but does that
          make me a slut? No.
               (beat)
          A slut is someone who sleeps around, or
          trades sex to get what she wants. Like
          when you slept with that goober to get
          him to write your English paper.

                    MILLY
          I'm not the slut!

                    MYTH MISTRESS
          And Santa's real! The shoe fits, psycho-
          bitch.

                    MILLY
          I hate you! I hate you! I'm sure I'm
          not the only one who hates you. I hope
          you die! I hope your fans turn on you
          and destroy you!

Milly storms out as the video ends.

                    MYTH MISTRESS
               (re the video)
          That was Milly, everybody. Still the
          biggest dork on campus... Hope you
          enjoyed watching, "The Legend of Milly,"
          as I did making it.
               (beat)
          Remember, keep sending in your urban myth
          and legend videos! We'll show as many of
          them as possible. But, right now let's
          get started with a short scary myth while
          I finish getting ready.

She clicks on a link and a video plays.

                                        CUT TO THE MYTH:

INT. FAMILY ROOM - NIGHT

An adolescent BABYSITTER talks into her cell phone.

                    BABYSITTER
          No, the kids are fine. They're both
          still sleeping.

INT. MOVIE THEATER LOBBY - SAME TIME

The MOTHER talks to the babysitter. The FATHER stands next
to her listening in.

CROSSCUT AS NEEDED

Father points to his watch.

                    FATHER
          What's going on, the movie is about to
          start.

                    MOTHER
          If the kids are okay, why did you call,
          Becky?

                    BABYSITTER
          I just wanted to know if it's okay for me
          to cover up the clown statue in the
          family room with a sheet?

                    MOTHER
          What clown statue?

                    BABYSITTER
          The one over by the window.

A five-foot clown stands in the corner, eyes staring blankly
at the babysitter.

                    MOTHER
          What?

                    BABYSITTER
          I mean, it's not that I don't appreciate
          your taste in art. But, like, it just
          freaks me out! The eyes follow me all
          over the room.

Concerned by his wife's expression.

                    FATHER
          What is it? What's going on?

                    BABYSITTER
          Like, it's totally staring at me now.

INT. MOVIE THEATER LOBBY - CONTINUOUS

                    MOTHER
          She says there's a clown statue in the
          family room staring at her.

The father grabs the phone out of her hand, panicked.

                    FATHER
          Grab the kids and get out of the house.

                    BABYSITTER
          What?

                    FATHER
          Just do it! Run for your life. I'll
          call the police.

                    BABYSITTER
          Why?

                    FATHER
          We don't have a clown statue!

The babysitter screams.

The father takes out his phone and dials 911. They both hear
screams coming through the mother's phone.

INT. FAMILY ROOM - CONTINUOUS

The babysitter runs for her life screaming.

The clown pursues her with a huge knife zigzagging through
the room.

She looks back. WHAM face-first into the wall.

The clown spins her around. She screams.

He buries the knife in the top of her head watching the tears
run down her face as her life slowly slips away.

                    BABYSITTER
          Why...

INT. MYTH BUNKER - CONTINUOUS

                    MYTH MISTRESS
          A killer clown. Nice! Good way to start
          tonight's Halloween live stream event!
          Some people love clowns. Others are
          scared silly of them. The urban legend
          of the clown statue falls into the scary
          category.

                    MYTH MISTRESS (CONT'D)
          It's been making the internet rounds for
          decades. Probably longer. And even
          though this story has never proven to be
          real, tales of killer clowns are based in
          fact... like all good legends... but it
          IS an urban myth. Or it may not be...
          who really knows for sure?

She turns to the camera behind her.

                    MYTH MISTRESS (cont'd)
          The best-known killer clown is John Wayne
          Gacy. Google it. During the mid-1970s,
          he murdered 33 people. The media dubbed
          him the "killer clown" because he hosted
          neighborhood parties dressed as a clown.
          That's where he found his victims.
               (beat)
          But who really knows if this clown statue
          story is true? That's why myths and
          legends are so much fun. I'd be scared
          shitless if a killer stood in my room
          staring at me! Clown or not. Eww...
          that's just creepy.

Milly bursts through the door.

                    MILLY
          YOU'LL NEVER GUESS WHAT HAPPENED!

                    MYTH MISTRESS
          SHIT! You scared the pee out of me!

                    MILLY
          Everyone is talking about it!

                    MYTH MISTRESS
          WTF, Milly! I told you NOT to come in
          here! You are now part of my live stream
          event AGAIN. For which you will receive
          NO compensation.

Milly looks around clueless.

                    MYTH MISTRESS (cont'd)
          So...
               (waiting)
          What is everyone talking about?

                    MILLY
          A psychic on 'Ellen' predicted there will
          be mass murder on a college campus during
          All Hallow's Eve!

The Myth Mistress looks into the camera.

                    MYTH MISTRESS
          That's pretty vague. Plus it sounds like
          the plot of a horror movie! Like many
          urban legends...

                    MILLY
          The psychic foretold the murders would
          take place at a large University that
          starts with the letter 'M' or 'W' and is
          in the Big 10 or Big 12 conference.
          Also, get this, she said the killer will
          be dressed as Little Bo Peep. That's
          pretty damn specific!

                    MYTH MISTRESS
               (looking back at Milly)
          I thought I had enlightened you. That IS
          an Urban Myth... I posted it on my
          website. It even has a name... The Bo
          Peep Killer.

                    MILLY
          Except this really happened. The entire
          world saw the prediction on TV.

                    MYTH MISTRESS
          Nothing happened. It's not going to
          happen. And Bloody Mary is not going to
          appear when you say her name three times
          in the bathroom mirror! Now, go away.
          And stop being a dumbass.

The Myth Mistress turns back to her monitors.

                    MILLY
          Don't speak to me like I'm a moron! You
          always do that! I hate it!
               (under her breath)
          You think you're so cool... You're gonna
          regret ever knowing me.

                    MYTH MISTRESS
          I already do...

Milly sulks away.

                    MYTH MISTRESS (cont'd)
               (into the camera)
          I've known Milly for far too long. If
          you haven't noticed, she's a couple of
          prescriptions short of not being psycho!
          But I must say, her complete lack of
          common sense IS impressive!

She searches the screen for more video files.

                    MYTH MISTRESS (cont'd)
          Anyway, let's see what mystery myth lies
          in this next video... and when we come
          back I'll be streaming from the first
          party of the evening.

The Myth Mistress clicks on the next video message.

An OLD LADY talks on the screen as the Myth Mistress watches.

                    OLD LADY
          This is a personal first-hand account...

                    MYTH MISTRESS
          Wow! I never had a first-hand account
          before.

                    OLD LADY
          It happened in 1952. I'll never forget
          how scared I was when my roommate told it
          to me.

                    MYTH MISTRESS
          Okay, there it is... not a real first-
          hand account, but a story from someone
          else who heard it from a friend who,
          heard from a... you get the geest.

                    OLD LADY
          Late one Friday night, Cindy was in her
          dorm room when she heard a gurgling moan
          coming from down the hallway.

                                        CUT TO THE MYTH:

INT. DORM - BEDROOM - NIGHT

Cindy lays in bed, frozen with fear, heart pounding. Every
time the moans stop there is a dragging sound. Over and over
- moan, drag, moan, drag...

Cindy shakes beneath the covers. The dragging grows louder
and louder, coming closer and closer stopping outside her
door.

A BANG on the door sends Cindy flying into the closet,
terrified.

Something scratches on the door.

Cindy doesn't move. Doesn't breathe. The scratching
continues. She covers her ears. It gets louder and louder.
She buries herself deeper and deeper in dirty laundry.

INT. DORM - BEDROOM - MORNING

Cindy jerks awake. She listens. Nothing. She eases her way out of the closet toward the front door, listening for any noise.

Too frightened to open the door, she rushes to the window to find help.

A mailman walks beneath her second-story window.

> CINDY
> HELP ME! HELP ME, PLEASE!

The mailman sees her then rushes inside.

Cindy hears his footsteps coming up the stairs and down the hallway.

Her breathing gets heavier and heavier as the footsteps grow nearer... then stop.

> CINDY (cont'd)
> Is that you? What's wrong?
>   (silence)
> Please answer me!

> MAILMAN (O.C.)
> Everything is okay. Just stay in your
> room. I'll get the police.

> CINDY
> POLICE! Why? What happened? Don't
> leave!

> MAILMAN
> Nothing's wrong. Just stay in your room
> and don't come out!

INT. DORM - OUTSIDE CINDY'S DOOR - CONTINUOUS

The doorknob turns. Cindy's face peers through a small opening.

She sees the mailman's pale face, his eyes wide with terror.

> MAILMAN
> Don't look down.

She does and screams. Her roommate is dead at her feet in a pool of blood, hatchet buried in her head.

Cindy opens the door in horror to see the deep scratches in the wood, her friend's nails worn down to bloody stumps, and the bloody trail where she dragged herself down the hallway hoping to be saved.

INT. MYTH BUNKER - NIGHT

The Myth Mistress looks into the camera.

                    MYTH MISTRESS
          As a college student, I can appreciate
          that story. I'm mean, c'mon, you met
          Milly... if I had an ax in my head she'd
          leave me outside for sure. Hell, she'd
          be the one that put it there!
                    (beat)
          But, seriously, like all the others so
          far, it's an urban myth. You see
          variations of it all over the internet.
          But a little old lady telling the story
          made this one different.
                    (beat)
          As you can see, I'm still in the Myth
          Bunker... I swear I'm heading to my first
          party of the night at the Sig Chi house
          right now. Keep an eye out for me... and
          Milly's serial killer!

A SCREEN TIME ALERT pops up on the center monitor.

                    MYTH MISTRESS (cont'd)
          Oh, shit, one of you is calling me...
          guess I'll stay a little longer...

She clicks on it. AMY appears on the monitor.

                    MYTH MISTRESS (cont'd)
          You got the Myth Mistress. What's your
          question?

                    AMY
          Hi, Myth Mistress. Happy Halloween! I
          love your interactive site.

                    MYTH MISTRESS
          Ah, thank you. Do you have a question
          for me?

                    AMY
          I wanted to ask about the "Old Hag
          Syndrome."

                    MYTH MISTRESS
          For those of you who don't know, she's
          not talking about Milly.

                    MYTH MISTRESS (CONT'D)
          (beat)
     The myth of the Old Hag finds its origins
     in folklore, particularly in
     Newfoundland, though variations of the
     story are present throughout the world.
     Tales of an old witch maliciously sitting
     on the chests of her victims while they
     lay in bed at night - when all dark and
     evil things happen.

                    AMY
     Yeah, and what had been a peaceful sleep
     turned into a waking nightmare. I was
     shocked awake, unable to move, and
     overwhelmed by a sense of evil. So, was
     it real?

                    MYTH MISTRESS
     While it sounds like a run-of-the-mill
     urban legend, the curious thing about the
     "Old Hag Syndrome" is that it is a highly
     reported phenomenon. People around the
     world have claimed to have woken up in
     terror, paralyzed, and often seeing or
     hearing things such as eyes in the
     darkness or the sound of footsteps. Even
     dark figures looming over their bodies.

                    AMY
     So, it's more than just sleep paralysis?

                    MYTH MISTRESS
     What do you think, gang? Is the old hag
     just doing what a wicked witch does?
          (beat)
     Or has the global pervasiveness of these
     experiences elevated the Old Hag Syndrome
     to something beyond urban legend?

                    AMY
     I believe in the paranormal... witches,
     demons, spirits, even aliens.

                    MYTH MISTRESS
     That's what is great about us! We all
     believe! And people have reported
     similar experiences without the
     paralysis.
          (beat)
     The commonality of every reporting and
     the hallucinations leaving almost
     everyone with a sense of evil... is very
     interesting.

MYTH MISTRESS (CONT'D)
Scientists and paranormal enthusiasts may
be at odds about what causes the Old Hag
Syndrome, but one simple truth may be
enough to keep you up at night - Whatever
the cause, it does exist. Thanks, Amy!
(beat)
Leave your comments on the page everybody
and let me know what you think.

The Myth Mistress searches for another video.

MYTH MISTRESS (cont'd)
For all you party people out there
waiting for me, I swear I'm leaving!

Seeing one titled, "The Mirror," she clicks on it. A MAN
appears holding a mirror covered in a black veil.

MIRROR MAN
Do you know why Jews cover all mirrors in
the house for a mourning period of seven
days after someone dies?
(beat)
Whenever a soul leaves this world, it
creates a vacuum, one that is prone to be
filled by dark forces. All types of evil
spirits and demons visit a family in
mourning looking to fill that void. And
so the house of mourning, the place where
the loss is felt the most, is a magnet
for evil spirits. These demons cannot be
seen by the naked eye. But when looking
in a mirror, you may catch a glimpse of
their reflection in the background. The
question is... are these evil spirits
just reflections of our inner demons? Or
real ones? And can they possess us? Or
is it all bubbe meise - an old wives'
tale?

Myth Mistress stops the video.

MYTH MISTRESS (V.O.)
Oooo creepy, dude. As for inner demons,
you can see those on Twitter, you don't
need a mirror. Seeing ghosts and being
possessed by them... hmmm... it's not for
me to say.

Turning on her iPhone 11 pro, she secures it to her SMOVE
steady-cam stabilizing stick, then talks into it while
walking toward the door.

                    MYTH MISTRESS
          See? I'm leaving folks. But one last
          thing... mirrors in a dark room with
          little or no light could be a dangerous
          thing. In my opinion. And viewing a
          mirror by candlelight might also be
          dangerous if myths and legends are to be
          believed.
                    (thinking)
          One such legend says that viewing a
          mirror by candlelight will show you your
          reflection - and that of any entities
          inhabiting your home, be they ghosts or
          otherwise.

She walks out the door and down the hall.

                    MYTH MISTRESS (cont'd)
          Needless to say, once you become aware of
          them, they also become aware of you...
          and odds are good that they won't be
          friendly. If **YOU** believe in such things.

The Myth Mistress clicks the video link on her phone.

                    MYTH MISTRESS (cont'd)
          Here's the rest of Mirror Man's story.

                    MIRROR MAN
          What I'm about to tell you is a true
          story about a magic mirror that was first
          documented in a traveling show called,
          "The Carnival of Oddities and Freaks," in
          the 1930s.

                                        CUT TO THE MYTH:

EXT. STAGE IN FRONT OF A BIG TENT - NIGHT

PEOPLE dressed in thirties attire mill around in front of a
large tent holding the main attractions.

                    BARKER
          Come see the breathtaking freaks, the
          unnerving creatures captured in the
          darkest forests and deepest seas... snake
          men, bearded ladies, mermaids, and more!
          See them all for only two bits.
                    (beat)
          Peer into our magic looking glass... if
          you dare. Hold it, if you like, make
          faces in it, watch it make faces at you,
          be our guest. But beware... you might be
          frightened by what you see!
                    (beat)

                    BARKER (CONT'D)
          Come be amazed, just one-quarter of a
          dollar, if you possess the courage to
          confront the spirits of the mirror!
                    (beat)
          The only caveat being you do so solely at
          your own risk.

One FAT LADY steps up with her quarter.

                    FAT LADY
          What does it do?

                    BARKER
          What does it do, madam? It reflects.

                    FAT LADY
          But what will I see if I pay to look into
          it?

OTHERS gather around, curious.

                    BARKER
          It could be a reflection of your soul.
          Your future, perhaps. Some see demons,
          or the dead milling about in limbo,
          spirits of the deceased... others report
          seeing into another dimension filled with
          knowledge from past, present, and future.
          Others see reflections not their own.

One MAN waves his arms, bellowing...

                    MAN
          Hell no! I ain't payin' for that!

                    BARKER
          Are there brave ones among you?!

OTHERS pursed their lips and squint, weighing the pros and
cons.

                    FAT LADY
          I want to see my future. After my diet.
          Will it show me that version of myself?

                    BARKER
          It may, madam. Keep those good thoughts.
          Whatever it is you do see, do not destroy
          the mirror or it will release the evil
          lurking within onto this plane.

This gives her a momentary cause for hesitation.

                    BARKER (cont'd)
          Never fear, madam, we have men standing
          beside the mirror to prevent that from
          happening.

INT. TENT - MOMENTS LATER

The fat lady enters the large tent and follows the signs for
all the cordoned-off rooms. Seeing the "Mirror Room" sign,
she enters.

MIRROR ROOM - CONTINUOUS

Stepping into the darkness, she sees a mirror illuminated
only by candles hanging from heavy wires, and covered by a
dark veil. LARGE WORKERS stand on both sides of it.

She wastes no time ripping off the veil with anticipation and
excitement.

Gazing into the glinting dark glass her expression changes to
horror, her eyes widen from shock. She screams and flees the
room.

EXT. TENT - SECONDS LATER

Fleeing the tent, she pushes her way quickly through the
CROWD, still horrified. The barker shouts to her.

                    BARKER
          So, madam, are you happy with what you
          saw?

                    FAT LADY
          NOT AT ALL! That mirror is evil!

                    BARKER
          What did it show you?

INT. MIRROR ROOM - SECONDS AGO

The fat lady stands in front of the mirror. A blurry figure
comes into focus - a terrifying reflection of her decomposing
corpse staring back at her.

                    FAT LADY (V.O.)
          A rotting corpse. MINE! And it was
          staring at me like it knew me!

RETURN TO SCENE

The fat lady screams, reliving the vision in her mind.

                    FAT LADY
          I should not have done that. I need to
          be on my knees praying to God!

The lady disappears into the crowd as they eagerly push
forward, money in hand.

                    BARKER
          You heard her, folks. It's a dark and
          evil mirror. Say a prayer and take the
          dare! See what the mirror has in store
          for you!

PEOPLE gasp and whisper. OTHERS buy tickets.

MONTAGE OF VARIOUS PATRONS' REFECTIONS

A SMALL MAN'S face smiles eerily back at him, it warps,
distorts, and twists with an evil grin freaking him out.

A WOMAN holding a CHILD sees four shadowy entities around
them, all touching and stroking the youngster. She screams
and runs away.

A YOUNG COUPLE sees the reflection of themselves fifty years
later in life, smiling and happy. They kiss. Their
refections watch and smile like they were remembering the
past.

A swirling black mass with DEATH riding a horse surrounded by
lightning, volcanos, and crashing waves terrifies an ELDERLY
WOMAN.

A large and IMPOSING MAN staggers backward from the mirror,
yelling a string of profanities as a person, who looks
exactly like him, peers around from behind his reflection,
shakes his head, then walks away.

                    IMPOSING MAN
          Holy fucking shit!

A SAD LADY sees her HUSBAND walk toward her. He places his
hand on his side of the mirror, his eyes beg for her touch.

She presses her palm to his instantly transforming her
husband into a DEMON still connected to her by their palms.

She screams yanking her hand back. But her palm print
remains in the demon's hand.

She violently rubs her palm print trying to get it off the
mirror. The demon laughs as her own corpse appears by his
side.

The sad lady steps back. Removing her crucifix, she steps
forward, boldly placing it on the mirror.

                    SAD LADY
          Release me or die when I smash this
          mirror!

The two large guards step up and pull her away.

                    GUARD #1
          You can't do that. It will release the
          demon.

She holds out her crucifix and shouts.

                    SAD LADY
          RELEASE ME! IN THE NAME OF GOD, I
          COMMAND YOU! GOD COMMANDS YOU!

The demon laughs as her palm fades. As it disappears it
mouths the words...

                    DEMON
               (mouthing the words)
          I'll be waiting for you...

EXT. PARANORMAL MUSEUM - DAY - 1977

The COUPLE carries the mirror shrouded in a black veil up to
a building with a sign that reads...

ODD COUPLE'S MUSEUM OF THE PARANORMAL ESTABLISHED 1952.

                    MIRROR MAN (V.O.)
          Stories of the mirror faded until the
          1970s when a couple brought it to a
          paranormal museum.

INT. PARANORMAL MUSEUM - LATER

The two couples sit in a circle looking at the veiled mirror.
SAM and MARY, (30s), the mirror's owners, tell their stories
to DAN and BETTY, (50s), the owners of the museum.

                    SAM
          Every day our cats were sitting in the
          chair at the far end of the living room,
          doing that hilarious head-bobble thing
          they do when they are watching something
          happen outside.
               (beat)
          That's when I realized not only do they
          never sit in the same chair together, but
          they weren't looking out the window.

                    SAM (CONT'D)
They were staring at the mirror... its
veil was lying on the floor.

                    MARY
It really was creepy.

                    SAM
Every night I'd cover it. Every morning
we'd see the unveiled mirror glinting in
the sunlight by the window.

                    MARY
The mirror was uncovering itself.

                    DAN
How do you know it wasn't the cats?

                    MARY
They kept their distance.

                    SAM
They'd stare at it, mesmerized, but never
get very close to it. It spooked them.

                    MARY
We had a party once and let our friends
look into it. The ones that wanted to.

                    SAM
One woman, who said she was a skeptic,
gave it a try.

                                        CUT TO:

INT. HOUSE - NIGHT

The SKEPTIC's evil reflection leans forward and speaks.

                    REFLECTION
You will die on a warm summer day... I
won't say which one... just to keep you
guessing... but you have sixty thousand
hours... give or take, until the day you
die...

The reflection laughs. The Skeptic is unnerved.

RETURN TO SCENE

                    SAM
She said her reflection told her when she
would die. Even though we all saw her
reflection never changed. It's mouth
never moved.

                    MARY
          And nobody heard anything. It really
          upset her.

                    BETTY
          What happened to her?

                    MARY
          Nothing.

                    SAM
          Yet...

                    MARY
          Throughout the rest of the night, our
          friend's stories were twice as creepy as
          that, if not more so.

                    SAM
          It became clear the mirror affected its
          surroundings and our friends.

                    MARY
          Many of the people who viewed the mirror
          died mysterious deaths or committed
          suicide since that night.

                    BETTY
          That's awful. I'm so sorry.

                    DAN
          You want to take a look into the mirror,
          hun? Give it a go?

                    BETTY
          I'm game if you are.

Dan holds up the mirror for her.

                    BETTY (cont'd)
          Oh, my God!

                    DAN
          What is it? What do you see?

                    BETTY
          People milling around the room.

Betty looks behind her to make sure the room was empty. It
is. She looks back into the mirror.

                    MARY
          The power it has is... unnatural.

                    SAM
          At least three separate friends saw a
          "black mass" hovering over their left
          shoulder, while others claimed to see
          dead relatives or small children.

                    MARY
          It became pretty easy to see that the
          mirror was affected by all the attention.
          It took over our lives. Nobody will come
          over anymore. It changed everything for
          the worse. That's why we brought it to
          you.

                    SAM
          So, fair warning.

                    DAN
          What do you think, Betty?

                    BETTY
          Let's buy it!

                    SAM
          Okay, don't say we didn't warn you.

                    BETTY
          Yeah, complain if you make us rich!

PARANORMAL MUSEUM - DAY

People mill about checking out all the "haunted objects."
There's a line waiting to take their turn with the mirror.
Many are horrified, leaving quickly, others laugh and joke.

Dan and Betty see items on the shelves move by themselves.

                    BETTY
          It's like the darkness in the mirror acts
          as a battery.

                    DAN
          Yeah, and everything's getting "juiced."

INT. PARANORMAL MUSEUM - EVENING

Dan and Betty close the museum and lock the doors. They
don't notice items on shelves moving, or the mirror glowing
as evil faces and shadows move in and out.

PARANORMAL MUSEUM - LATE NIGHT

Chaos in the museum causes damage and havoc. Cursed
instruments play themselves.

Objects float around the room like someone is carrying them.

The action intensifies until the museum bursts into flames.

Apparitions, spirits, shadow people, even corpses, escape from the flaming mirror.

EXT. COLLEGE CAMPUS - NIGHT

The video ends on the Myth Mistress' cell phone screen at the end of her SMOVE steady-cam stick as she walks and talks.

> MYTH MISTRESS
> Wow! Nice story Mirror Man.
> (beat)
> There is some precedence for a kind of "storage" like this. Throughout history, some cultures believed that mirrors had the power to capture energy, even souls. Serbo-Croatian cultures would bury their dead with a mirror to trap the soul of the deceased, preventing it from wandering the Earth for the rest of eternity.

She stops and adjusts herself.

> MYTH MISTRESS (cont'd)
> Wow, it's hard to walk and talk in knee-high leather boots with six-inch stiletto heels.

She adjusts to a wider shot to show her surroundings.

> MYTH MISTRESS (cont'd)
> As you can see, I haven't made it to the party. But I'm on campus... come get me, Little Bo Peep! What was I talking about?

Comments pop up.

INSERT: MIRRORS. GHOSTS. CAPTURING DEMONS.

> MYTH MISTRESS
> oh, yeah... mirrors were believed to act as a kind of portal to the "spiritual realm", and used to capture and contain evil spirits.
> (looking around)
> Modern science lends some credibility to the claim that mirrors can store energy. In fact, a lot of research into green energy is invested in the use of mirrors to trap and contain sunlight.

                    MYTH MISTRESS (CONT'D)
               (looking back and forth)
          So, if mirrors can store sunlight, who
          are we to say they can't store ghosts,
          demons, even memories because those are
          all just different forms of energy.
               (trying not to laugh)
          But like most folklore, it's easy to
          dismiss these as tales told by uneducated
          superstitious people.

She holds the SMOVE steady-cam stick higher to reveal her
surroundings.

                    MYTH MISTRESS (cont'd)
          Get a load of this...

Dozens of WOMEN and MEN dressed in Little Bo Peep costumes.

                    MYTH MISTRESS (cont'd) (O.C.)
          Looks like all these people heard the
          same story Milly did.

Turns the camera back to herself.

                    MYTH MISTRESS (cont'd)
          Okay, peeps, I need to jet... which ain't
          easy dressed like this.
               (beat)
          So here's a nice ghost story for you. We
          believe in ghosts, don't we, gang? We
          just saw some in the mirror!

A young FEMALE speaks into a webcam.

                    FEMALE
          Hey, Myth Mistress, have you ever dreamed
          of a ghost... or a stranger speaking to
          you in your sleep? Was it really a
          dream? Or are the dead trying to
          communicate with you?
               (beat)
          This actually happened to my aunt
          Sharon's best friend's boyfriend. It was
          in the papers.

The Myth Mistress speaks over the video.

                    MYTH MISTRESS
          Like I said, it's always a friend of a
          friend and it's always in the paper... Or
          online somewhere, but you can never find
          it. Or it's fake.

Images of ghost sightings from across the world play screen.

                    FEMALE (V.O.)
          Most ancient cultures believed in ghosts
          and spirits. Some still believe today.
          But many Americans doubt the existence of
          spirits that dwell among the living. But
          did you know in California when selling a
          house you're required to disclose any
          deaths that have taken place there?

Back to the female speaking into the camera.

                    FEMALE
          Did you ever wonder why people drown in
          the same spot or die at the same curve in
          the road? The untimely deaths leave
          behind cursed spirits unable to move on.
          So, they dwell at that spot for
          eternity... or until they find another
          soul to replace them. What I'm about to
          tell you is a true story.

                                        CUT TO THE MYTH:

EXT. LAKE - BOAT DOCK - WALKWAY - DAY

Two GIRLS fight frantically to keep their heads above water.

Each time they come up something pulls them under.

They gasp for air each time they emerge...

Shriek each time they're pulled down.

A man, SAM, sees this and dives in to save them.

He resurfaces with girl one under his arm and swims her to
the dock.

He takes a deep breath and dives for the other... Popping up
moments later with her in tow.

The first girl coughs as the second rolls onto the dock
spewing water out of her lungs.

                    GIRL #1
          Something was pulling on my leg.

                    GIRL #2
          Mine, too!

   Sam climbs onto the dock.

                    SAM
          There are a lot of old dead trees at the
          bottom of this lake. You got stuck in a
          branch or something.

                    GIRL #2
          That was no tree!

                    GIRL #1
          It was a hand! I felt it!

                    GIRL #2
          It had me by the ankle.

                    GIRL #1
          I'm never swimming here again!

                    SAM
          No one could hold their breath that long.
          I know you're scared, but there's nothing
          down there.

                    GIRL #1
          Nothing alive!

Terrified, the girls run to the shore.

INT. SAM'S BEDROOM - NIGHT

Sam sleeps peacefully in his bed.

SAM'S DREAM - SAME TIME

A beautiful ASIAN WOMAN walks toward Sam, who's standing at
the foot of his bed.

                    ASIAN WOMAN
          You save young ones from death...

Sam smiles as she approaches.

                    ASIAN WOMAN (cont'd)
          You hero man...

She rubs against him seductively.

                    ASIAN WOMAN (cont'd)
          You know what I do to you, hero man?

She pushes Sam on the bed then jumps on top of him.

                    ASIAN WOMAN (cont'd)
          I show you!

SAM'S DREAM - UNDERWATER

FLASH. Sam is underwater struggling to reach the surface.
He can't breathe. Looking down he sees...

The woman floating beneath him, reaching up for him.

SAM'S DREAM - BACK IN BEDROOM

FLASH. Sam is back in bed with the woman. She lays on top
of him holding down his arms. He squirms to free himself
from her crushing weight.

> ASIAN WOMAN
> You had no business saving those girls.
> Now you gonna be my hero man.

FLASH. The woman is gone.

INT. BEDROOM - REALITY

Sam shoots up, clutching his chest, fighting to breathe.

Both Sam, and the bed, are soaking wet.

INT. SAM'S LIVING ROOM - THE NEXT EVENING

Sam hands JOHN a drink.

> SAM
> The woman in my dream... she was Chinese,
> I think. Really beautiful... laying on
> top of me--

> JOHN
> I should be so lucky!

> SAM
> No, it was terrifying. I couldn't move.
> I couldn't breathe. And when I woke up,
> I was wet! The bed was soaked.
> Everything was drenched.

> JOHN
> Yeah, I used to have those kinds of
> dreams, too. When I was thirteen!

> SAM
> No, man, this was no wet dream. I'm
> serious. She even left wet footprints
> out of the room.

> JOHN
> Damn, dude! Are you sure you were awake?
> No way there were footprints! Unless...

                    SAM
          There's no way a person in my dreams can
          leave footprints PERIOD!

                    JOHN
          It could be a haunting.

                    SAM
          I don't believe in that paranormal stuff.
          But... it was so real.

                    JOHN
          Well, all I know is water in a dream is a
          symbol of sexual repression. Or
          something like that. I read it on some
          dream website.

                    SAM
          I believe in that less than ghosts.

                    JOHN
          All I can say, dude, is beautiful wet
          Asian chicks can lay on me in dreams any
          time.

                    SAM
          You don't want a dream like this.

The doorbell rings. Sam moves to the door and opens it.

                    SAM (cont'd)
          You! Who are you? Why are you here?
          What do you want from me?

John sees a soaking wet Asian woman standing in front of Sam.

                    JOHN
          Dream, huh? No wonder everything was
          wet. Why did you make up the whole ghost
          story?

                    SAM
          I didn't! Don't leave!

                    JOHN
          Sure, man. Whatever. See you later,
          buddy.
               (sarcastically)
          Sweet dreams!

John walks out the door past the woman.

                    SAM
          Why are you wet?

                    ASIAN WOMAN
          Ask me in... hero man.

Curiosity and fear paralyze him momentarily.

                    SAM
          I may regret this... but sure please...
          come in.

She moves past him toward the bedroom.

                    SAM (cont'd)
          Have we met before?

                    ASIAN WOMAN
          Last night.

                    SAM
          No. I mean... last night? How is that
          possible?

She motions to him from the bedroom doorway.

                    ASIAN WOMAN
          Join me and find out.

                    SAM
          But I don't know you. I didn't even
          think you were real.

                    ASIAN WOMAN
          Come find out how real.

She disappears into the room. Sam hesitates.

INT. SAM'S BEDROOM - A MINUTE LATER

Sam enters a bit anxious.

Her clothes are on the floor. She is under the covers.

Sam's senses scream warnings to his brain.

                    SAM
          No. I can't. This isn't happening.

                    ASIAN WOMAN
          Come...

Sam's uncontrollably drawn to her. Powerless to resist. He
slowly removes his clothes and joins her under the blankets.

She mounts him and strokes his face.

                    ASIAN WOMAN (cont'd)
              You are mine now...

The room begins to spin. His vision blurs.

He grabs his pounding head, eyes clinched until...

The spinning stops. His eyes meet her empty black stare.

She squeezes his neck with both hands.

Sam struggles to free himself, to breathe, to move.

She places her mouth on his, sucking his breath until he
passes out.

IN HIS HEAD

FLASH. He's back underwater. Blackness turns blue. A light
illuminates his surroundings. His arms and legs flail,
fighting to reach the surface.

But the more he struggles the deeper he sinks.

Lack of air crushes him like a lead suit. He looks beneath
him. The nude woman pulls him by his legs deeper and deeper
into the water.

                    ASIAN WOMAN
              The lives you saved belonged to me... now
              your life is mine.

Sam screams. Water fills his lungs.

Deeper and deeper he sinks, fighting to free himself as the
blackness overtakes him once more.

INT. SAM'S BEDROOM - MORNING

Sam shoots out of bed choking up water.

                    SAM
              What the hell! This shit can't be real!

He rubs his chest.

A flash of movement frightens him. He spins, quickly
searching the room for the woman.

She is inside the mirror, but he doesn't see her.

                    SAM (cont'd)
              What the hell is happening to me?

EXT. LAKE - BOAT DOCK - BAIT SHOP - LATER

An old CHINESE MAN stands behind the counter. Sam enters.

                    OLD CHINESE MAN
          Can I help you, mister?
              (recognizing him)
          Hey, you are the man who saved those two
          girls.

                    SAM
          Yeah, that was me.

                    OLD CHINESE MAN
          What can I do for you, hero man?

                    SAM
          What did you call me?

                    OLD CHINESE MAN
          You are a hero.

                    SAM
          You said "hero man." Why?

                    OLD CHINESE MAN
          It is something we say in my country. No
          big deal.

                    SAM
          Maybe you can help me.
              (beat)
          A beautiful Chinese woman called me that
          in my dreams.

                    OLD CHINESE MAN
          We should all be so lucky.

                    SAM
          You don't understand. This woman showed
          up at my door the next night.

                    OLD CHINESE MAN
          Sounds like a dream come true. Why do
          you worry?

                    SAM
          She tried to kill me! Then I woke up all
          wet, the whole place was wet! My lungs
          were full of water.

The Chinese man flinches.

                    SAM (cont'd)
          What is it?

The old man shakes his head.

                    SAM (cont'd)
          Tell me! I don't know what to do.

                    OLD CHINESE MAN
          It's too late.

                    SAM
          Too late for what?

                    OLD CHINESE MAN
          You have been seduced by a succubus.
          There is nothing a living person can do
          to save you now.

                    SAM
          What the hell are you talking about?! A
          succubus?

                    OLD CHINESE MAN
          Female apparition.

                    SAM
          A ghost you mean?

                    OLD CHINESE MAN
          Ghost, specter, phantom, spook, figment
          of your imagination, however American
          minds can understand it.

                    SAM
          So you're saying a "ghost" walked out of
          my dreams, through my front door, and
          into my bed?

                    OLD CHINESE MAN
          If she was in physical form, she would
          have to be invited.
                    (off Sam's look)
          You invited her into your home?

                    SAM
          Yes, but I don't believe in any of this.

                    OLD CHINESE MAN
          The Chinese have known about the spirit
          realm for thousands of years. It is but
          one part of our world. But you Americans
          know nothing. Your minds do not believe,
          so your eyes do not see what is right in
          front of them.

                    SAM
          That's bullshit!

                    OLD CHINESE MAN
          Spirits of people who die unnatural
          deaths are confined to the place where
          they died until a replacement is found.

                    SAM
          Replacement?

                    OLD CHINESE MAN
          To be released, the confined spirit must
          find another soul to occupy the place of
          its death.

                    SAM
          That's nonsense!

                    OLD CHINESE MAN
          The spot where you saved those two girls
          there has been many deaths. The last one
          was a Chinese woman, very beautiful...
          except to one man. He pushed her into
          the water because he knew a spirit
          dwelled in that spot and would take her
          life.

                    SAM
          Then why the hell doesn't she haunt him?!

                    OLD CHINESE MAN
          It does not work that way. By saving
          those girls you stopped her from
          collecting a replacement soul. She did
          not move on and she blames you. She's
          attached to you so strongly she crossed
          over. You are not safe.

                    SAM
          What?! Screw that! Screw you! Screw
          all of this garbage.

Sam storms out of the shop.

EXT. BAIT SHOP - CONTINUOUS

Sam exits walking down the dock.

The Asian woman appears behind him and pushes him into the
water at the same spot where he saved the two girls.

Sam struggles to stay above water.

The Old Chinese man shanks his head, watching through the
window as Sam finally disappears beneath the surface.

The beautiful Asian woman, now free, walks down the dock fading into the horizon.

EXT. CAMPUS - LATER

The video continues on the Myth Mistress' cell phone screen at the end of her SMOVE steady-cam stick.

                         FEMALE
              This really happened. It was just one of
              a long string of deaths at the same spot
              in the lake where I grew up.

The Myth Mistress live streams herself walking across campus.

                         MYTH MISTRESS
              OMG, I love a good ghost story! That one
              was spooky. I never put that together.
              People dying in the same spot over and
              over. Interesting. So, is that the last
              death there... or will that dude kill
              someone else, and then they kill another,
              and so on, and so on? Only a priest
              knows... or a ghost.

LITTLE BO PEEP stalks Myth Mistress, taking care to stay in the shadows, eyeing her intently.

A COWBOY bumps into Bo Peep.

                         BO PEEP
              Watch it, fucker!

Bo Peep buries a large knife under the Cowboy's chin, blood spilling from his lips.

                         COWBOY
              Fuck, dude...

He drops to the ground, dead. Bo Peep continues on in the shadows behind Myth Mistress watching her doing her show.

                         MYTH MISTRESS
              If you believe in such things. It seems
              like the Chinese do have a lot of ghost
              stories, though.

Myth Mistress moves the camera showing her surroundings.

                         MYTH MISTRESS (cont'd)
              Hey, some of you guys did find me and...
              I didn't quite make it to the party. But
              I'm sure after this next video I'll be at
              the Sig Chi house, so keep watching.

                    MYTH MISTRESS (CONT'D)
          Better yet, meet me there, and get some
          free beer!

She clicks on a video and walks away. Full-screen video of
JILL speaking into her webcam plays on her iPhone screen.

                    JILL
          Hi, Myth Mistress, my name is Jill. This
          is not a story, well it is, but it's
          something that really happened to my best
          friend's cousin.

                                        CUT TO THE MYTH:

INT. BEDROOM - NIGHT

Several teenage GIRLS sit in a circle.

                    SALLY
          Truth or dare?

                    ANNE
          Truth.

                    SALLY
          What is your most embarrassing secret?

                    ANNE
          How can you ask me that?!

                    SALLY
          You chose truth, Anne! So spill.

Anne pouts.

                    PAM
          Just tell us already.

                    ANNE
          The first time I got my period was in the
          girls' showers in seventh grade. I saw
          the blood running down my legs and all
          over the shower floor. My mom never gave
          me 'the talk,' so I thought something bad
          was wrong. The other girls made fun of
          me!

                    PAM
          Bullshit! That happened in the movie
          "Carrie!"

                    SALLY
          Look, Anne, you started this, so you MUST
          tell us the truth about it.

                    OTHER GIRLS
Yeah...

                    ANNE
No way... I can't. It's my most
embarrassing moment for a reason! I take
dare. Give me dare.

                    SALLY
No!

                    ANNE
I'll do anything.

                    JANE
I have a good one.

                    SALLY
I want to hear it before I agree to let
her off the hook.

                    JANE
Old man Larson had narcolepsy and a weak
heart. He was so old they basically were
just waiting for him to die. His living
will stated that he was not to be
autopsied or embalmed for that reason.
     (pause)
So, he was to be buried in a large coffin
with a bell, in case he had been buried
alive and needed to be rescued.

                    DONNA
I heard they thought he was dead a bunch
of times, so that really saved him.

                    PAM
They found him last week unresponsive
with no pulse, so they buried him.

                    JANE
Leslie Jones was making out in the
cemetery last weekend and heard someone
ringing a bell near Old man Larson's
grave!

                    SALLY
Okay, Anne's dare is to go down to his
grave and wait to see if you hear him
ringing his bell.

                    ANNE
That can't be true... it's impossible.

                    PAM
          Then do it.

                    JANE
          Alone.

                    PAM
          Totally.

                    DONNA
          If she's alone, how will we know she
          didn't just go home?

Sally looks around searching for something. She grabs her
"Buffy The Vampire" commemorative stake.

                    SALLY
          Take this stake and stick it in the grave
          to prove you were there. If you cheat
          may the devil drag you to hell.

                    DONNA
          We'll all go down there together at
          sunrise to see if you really did it.

                    JANE
          And if you don't do it, we'll post nasty
          shit about you on Facebook.

                    ANNE
          I don't want to do this.

                    SALLY
          Okay.

Sally opens Facebook on her phone and speaks as she types.

                    SALLY (cont'd)
          We are playing truth and dare and Anne
          just confessed that she screwed sixty-two-
          year-old Coach Shepard.

                    ALL THE GIRLS
          Ewww...

                    SALLY
          She says grandpa sex is the best and she
          can't wait to do it again!

                    ANNE
          Okay, okay, I'm going. I'll be back for
          my next turn.

She grabs the stake and leaves.

EXT. CEMETERY - MIDNIGHT

It's dark and creepy. Anne is petrified, jumping at every
owl hoot and twig snap while stumbling around using her phone
to find Old man Larson's grave. She tries to whistle, but
her mouth is too dry.

                    ANNE
              (to herself)
         Just find the grave, put the stake in it
         and get the hell outta here before
         something happens!

Anne hears a faint bell ring in the distance. She screams.

INT. BEDROOM - DAWN

Anne runs into the room.

                    ANNE
         Why did you make me go to the cemetery
         alone?! I hate you!!

Donna jolts awake expecting to see Anne. She is not there.

                    DONNA
         Oh, shit! Oh, shit! Oh, shit! Wake up!
         Something's happened to Anne.

They all wake up and look around. No sign of Anne.

                    SALLY
         Calm down, Donna.

                    DONNA
         She was in my dream screaming at me for
         making her go there alone!

                    SALLY
         Nothing happened to that princess.

                    JANE
         I put a bell on his grave...

                    DONNA
         Oh, shit. You fuckin' bitch!

                    PAM
         We need to go find her.

The others agree.

                    JANE
         I bet she heard the bell and ran home
         like the scare little shit she is.

EXT. CEMETERY - DAWN

The girls spot Anne in the distance sitting slumped on a
grave.

                    PAM
          There she is.

                    JANE
          Is she sleeping?

They all run over to her. Anne's body is lifeless and pale.

                    DONNA
          Oh, my God, it was her ghost in my dream!
          She was angry we sent her out here
          because she died!

                    SALLY
          She's not dead.

Sally slaps Anne upside the head. Her body falls over
revealing that she staked herself to the grave and died from
fright. They scream.

                    PAM
          Is she...

Donna kneels over her body.

                    DONNA
          Yes!! She's dead!

They scream again and run away as fast as they can.

INT. SIG CHI HOUSE - LATER

The Myth Mistress continues her live stream event in the
middle of a Halloween party surrounded by MEN and WOMEN in
costume.

                    MYTH MISTRESS
          Wow. I vaguely recall a story about a
          girl who died of fright in a graveyard.
          Excuse me.

She downs her beer.

                    MYTH MISTRESS (cont'd)
          Ah... that's good. Free beer is the
          best.
               (beat)
          Scary urban legends are rarely factually
          verified but do reveal important truths
          about our deepest, darkest fears.

                    MYTH MISTRESS (cont'd)
          Embracing these fears by sharing them
          with a group is a way of confronting and
          coping with those things that scare us
          most. Plus, they're fun. That's why I
          built this site and why all...

She checks the viewer count. It reads 100,000.

                    MYTH MISTRESS (cont'd)
          One-hundred-thousand of you are spending
          your Halloween with me. Wow! Thanks for
          getting the word out. But we need to hit
          one million! C'mon, you guys can do it.
          Here, retweet this.

She takes a picture of FRAT DUDES dressed as Little Bo Peep
and tweets it.

                    MYTH MISTRESS (cont'd)
          You'd think frat dudes would like to be
          scared, too... not dress up like little
          girls...

She shows her audience all the Bo Peep dudes.

                    MYTH MISTRESS (cont'd)
          ...but then you'd be wrong. Let's ask
          one why.

She grabs the nearest BO PEEP DUDE.

                    MYTH MISTRESS (cont'd)
          Hey, there, stud, why are you dressed up
          like a little girl rather than a big
          scary thing?

                    DUDE
          What's scarier than a chick that will
          kill you?

                    MYTH MISTRESS
          Good point.
               (looking into the camera)
          There you have it. A common man on the
          street perspective... so to speak. The
          next member video from Sandy is about
          young lovers. Give us a break from evil
          mirrors, ghosts, and death.
               (afterthought)
          But be sure and stay tuned all night for
          all the Little Bo Peep intrigue!

                                        CUT TO THE MYTH:

EXT. HIGH SCHOOL GYMNASIUM - NIGHT

DANCE MUSIC wafts through the air. A High school sign reads
PROM NIGHT 2019.

A young couple, JIM BOY and LINDA LOU, dressed in "prom
night" attire, burst through the doors. They stop and
embrace passionately.

                    JIM BOY
          I love you, Linda Lou!

                                        DISSOLVE TO:

INT. BEDROOM AT THE RAMADA INN - LATER

The same two lovers embrace in the afterglow of their first
sexual encounter.

                    LINDA LOU
          I love you too, Jim Boy!

                    JIM BOY
          Linda Lou?

                    LINDA LOU
          Yes, Jim boy.

                    JIM BOY
          I'm worried--

                    LINDA LOU
          It didn't hurt.

                    JIM BOY
          Oh, not that... well, your screaming
          scared me a little at first, but that's
          not it...

Linda looks puzzled.

                    JIM BOY (cont'd)
          ...it's just that you're going to the
          east coast to study Art and I'll be here
          at State learning Animal Husbandry.

                    LINDA LOU
          Don't worry Jim Boy!

                    JIM BOY
          But--

                    LINDA LOU
          I just gave you my virginity, didn't I?

He smiles.

                    LINDA LOU (cont'd)
          Well, I wouldn't have done that if you
          weren't the most important thing in my
          life. I love you... I will always love
          you, I promise.

                    JIM BOY
          Then we'll always be together?

She nods and they are consumed by their passion.

EXT. BARNYARD - DAY

SUPER: 6 MONTHS LATER

Jim Boy slumps against the wall between the phone and a cow.
He holds the receiver in one hand and a soiled glove in the
other. Discouraged, he gazes at the large cow next to him
and hangs up the receiver.

INT. COLLEGE BOOKSTORE - SAME TIME

Linda Lou smiles at TWO PRETTY BOYS while waiting in line.

                    LINDA LOU
          Hey, there...

EXT. BARNYARD - DAY

Jim Boy stands next to a horse, one rubber glove... phone to
ear... discouraged again, he hangs up.

INT. FRAT HOUSE - THAT NIGHT

Linda Lou and SEVERAL HOT CHICKS enter a raging frat party.
FRAT boys everywhere. Linda cuts loose with the nearest one.

                    LINDA LOU
          I love college!

EXT. BARNYARD - DAY

Jim holds the phone, disappointed.

INT. FRAT HOUSE BEDROOM - NIGHT

Linda Lou lies on the bed. A BIG BUFF GUY stands over her.
She smiles coyly as she pulls him down on top of her.

EXT. BARNYARD - DAY

Jim Boy talks on the phone.

> JIM BOY
> Linda Lou, you said we'd always be
> together, but I haven't heard from you in
> over six months!

INT. LINDA LOU'S DORM ROOM - DAY

Linda Lou enters, her answering machine shows 15 in the
message window. She hits play.

> JIM BOY
> (on the answering machine)
> Linda Lou... our love--

CLICK, she deletes the message. The next message starts.

> JIM BOY (CONT'D)
> (on the answering machine)
> Linda Lou, I love you--

DELETE. The next one...

> JIM BOY (CONT'D)
> (on the answering machine)
> Linda Lou--

She deletes them all.

INT. FRAT HOUSE BEDROOM - LATER THAT NIGHT

Linda Lou snaps a selfie with a nude STUD. She hands the
stud the camera and kneels. The stud aims at his crotch.

INT. JIM BOY'S DORM ROOM - THE NEXT DAY

Jim Boy checks his emails. He smiles when he sees one from
Linda Lou. As he reads it his happiness fades.

INSERT: JIM BOY WE'RE THROUGH! GET OVER IT!

Jim Boy opens the attachments with dozens of sexual selfies
taken with all her different conquests. He is heartbroken...

He smiles, after devising a devious plan.

INT. LINDA LOU'S PARENT'S HOME - NIGHT

Linda's MOTHER opens her email.

> MOTHER
> Dad, we got an email from Linda.

She gasps. DAD moves to her.

                         DAD
               What is it dear?

He sees the pictures, not as attachments, but in the body of
the email below the message:

INSERT OF EMAIL: DEAR MOM AND DAD, COLLEGE IS SO MUCH FUN.
BIOLOGY IS MY FAVORITE SUBJECT. ALONG WITH ANATOMY! I'M
LEARNING SO MUCH. PLEASE SEND MONEY. LOVE, LINDA LOU.

EXT. CAMPUS - LATER THAT NIGHT

Myth Mistress walks across the campus still crowded with
PEOPLE in costumes, dozens of them are BO PEEPS, talking to
her viewers.

                    MYTH MISTRESS
               Jim Boy, huh? You gotta love those
               southern names. But I'll give it to
               him... he got his revenge.
                    (beat)
               In a sense, stories like that are
               commonly used to convince high school
               kids the futility of what they think is
               true love. But Linda Lou and Joe Bob, or
               Billy Bob, whatever the dude's name
               was... never really happened, I'm sure.
               And, not to be mean, but the Blair Witch
               isn't true either.
                    (beat)
               It COULD be true, that's why it works.
               But who knows for sure?

She holds up the steady-cam stick creating a wider view.

                    MYTH MISTRESS (cont'd)
               As you can see, I'm on my way to the
               Kappa Alpha Psi party for more free beer!
               Woo hoo!

A LARGE LITTLE BO PEEP rushes at her from behind.

Live Comments pop up on her screen.

**BEHIND YOU! LOOK OUT HE'S GOT A KNIFE! IT'S THE BO PEEP
KILLER! HE'S COMING UP BEHIND YOU!! RUN!! LITTLE BO PEEP
IS TRYING TO KILL YOU! YES, I AM GOING TO KILL YOU... BUT
NOT UNTIL MIDNIGHT.**

The Myth Mistress reads the comments then looks behind her to
see Bo Peep with a knife. She screams. He grabs her. She
struggles then yanks off his mask.

                    MYTH MISTRESS
               Damn it, Dan! You bastard!

DAN, (21) African American, laughs and bends the knife to
show her it's rubber.

                    DAN
          You said to come find you... Thought it
          would be cool to scare the shit out of
          you. It was.

                    MYTH MISTRESS
          Yeah, for you. And I guess everyone else
          watching. But damn, dude. That was a
          terrible thing to do to me.
               (into the phone)
          But I'm sure you all loved it. Now you
          can love this next video. I can't have
          any witnesses to what I'm about to do to
          this jackass!

She clicks on the next video post. DOUG speaks into a
camera.

                    DOUG
          Hey, Myth Mistress, I love your site...
          and you... you're hot.

While the video plays Myth Mistress punches Dan in the arm.
He chuckles.

                    MYTH MISTRESS
          Son of a bitch! You really scared me!

                    DAN
          If you saw the look on your face... You
          pretend to be this badass Dominatrix, but
          you looked like a frightened little girl.

                    MYTH MISTRESS
          Ha, ha, at least I didn't shit myself
          like you did last Halloween when I punked
          your ass!

                    DAN
          Yeah, payback's a bitch, huh?

                    MYTH MISTRESS
          Yeah, well, I'm sure my members got a
          kick out of it at least. I'm heading to
          your house's party... you coming?

                    DAN
          You go on, I got more people to "kill"
          thanks to the popularity of your site!

                    MYTH MISTRESS
          Loser...

She walks away. Dan pulls the mask back over his face
walking backward enjoying the view of her from behind.

He turns bumping into a SMALLER LITTLE BO PEEP.

                    DAN
          Nice costume.

Smaller Bo Peep buries a large knife in his gut.

                    SMALLER LITTLE BO PEEP
          She's mine, asshole.

Dan drops to his knees, blood streaming from his mouth.

                    DAN
          Oh, shit... your knife is real.

                    SMALLER LITTLE BO PEEP
          Duh...

Dan dies at Smaller Bo Peep's feet who steps over him
disappearing into the darkness.

CAMPUS - MOMENTS LATER

Myth Mistress walks toward the Kappa Alpha Psi house as Doug
continues on the video.

                    DOUG
          Anyway, the story was in the newspaper.
          It happened about ten years ago. My
          cousin's friend's girlfriend worked as an
          assistant to a big shot Hollywood
          Producer...

                                        CUT TO THE MYTH:

INT. FILM EXEC OFFICE - DAY

MARION KATZ, meticulously dressed, but showing many signs of
age, stress, and years of smoking, spins around in her chair
yelling into her headset.

                    MS KATZ
          Screw Stallone! News flash, he's old!
          We need a younger even dumber version of
          him... or Cruise... only taller.

She takes a hard pull on her cigarette.

                    MS KATZ (cont'd)
          And for god sake, none of those beta male
          millennial twinks you keep sending me!

                    MS KATZ (CONT'D)
          I'm looking for manly men, not
          androgynous twits. Someone who has
          testosterone!

A gangly, carelessly dressed, ASSISTANT enters clumsily with
a large stack of scripts, banging into everything.

MS Katz snaps her fingers pointing indiscriminately, wanting
something.

The Assistant picks up a pen. MS Katz waves it off and snaps
again, pointing. Still talking on the phone.

                    MS KATZ (cont'd)
               (to the caller)
          Yes, yes... that's good.

The Assistant thinks she's talking to her. MS Katz shakes
her head "no!"

She picks up a coffee cup. Katz waves it off snapping and
waving her finger wildly.

Frustrated, the Assistant looks around in confusion. She
grabs things: A bagel, nope, snap, a script, no, snap, snap.

MS Katz's intensity increases. She gets louder on the
phone, as her pointing becomes more frantic.

                    MS KATZ (cont'd)
          DON'T MAKE ME SUE YOUR ASS!

The Assistant grabs everything, stapler, staple remover, the
three-hole punch, fax machine. No, no, no, snap, snap, snap.

                    THE ASSISTANT
          What the hell do you want from me!?

                    MS KATZ
               (in phone calmly)
          I'll have to call you back, George.

She hangs up.

                    MS KATZ (cont'd)
          My car keys you nitwit! How are you
          going to be my secretary if you can't
          read my needs? You've got to stay one
          step ahead of me. Always!

                    ASSISTANT
          Okay. Number one, I'm not a nitwit. I
          graduated from Brown. Number two, I'm
          not your secretary, I'm your assistant.

                    MS KATZ
          Oh, grow up!

MS Katz mocks her by making little faces and noises.

                    ASSISTANT
          Number three... your keys aren't here
          because you sent Chip to wash your car.
          And number four - don't mock me! I hate
          it when you mock me!

                    MS KATZ
          Then don't be so damn mockable! I
          thought I sent that kid to wash my car
          like two days ago or something!

                    ASSISTANT
          It was an hour ago.

                    MS KATZ
          Whatever! Tell Biff he's fired.

                    ASSISTANT
          His name is Chip, and you can't fire him,
          he's an intern.

                    MS KATZ
          Then you're fired.

                    ASSISTANT
          You can't fire me, I'm the only one
          who'll put up with you. Everyone else
          prays for your painful demise.

                    MS KATZ
          I despise you!

                    ASSISTANT
          And I you!

                    MS KATZ
          Oh, drop dead!

                    ASSISTANT
          I get through the day just thinking about
          dancing on your grave.

                    MS KATZ
          Not bad. You're learning! I'm going to
          make an executive out of you yet.

The Assistant flops down on the sofa.

                    ASSISTANT
          I'm not sure I want to be one if it means
          being such a flaming bitch all the time.

                    MS KATZ
          Please! You sound like my grandmother.

                    ASSISTANT
          Your grandmother?

MS Katz fires up another cigarette, even though the first one
is still burning.

                    MS KATZ
          My grandmother, God bless her, was the
          sweetest, kindest most agreeable woman I
          ever knew.

The Assistant smiles.

                    MS KATZ (cont'd)
          My grandfather screwed her best friend
          and ran out on her. She worked as a
          cleaning lady for twenty-five years,
          where she was abused daily by her
          employer. Then my mother, who was a
          whore, dumped me on her and split. She
          died penniless the day before I graduated
          from high school, but... she was always
          nice.

                    ASSISTANT
          That's an awful story!

                    MS KATZ
          You listen to me. I didn't climb to the
          top of this dung heap by being sweet.
          Sometimes being a bitch is all that keeps
          you alive in this world. It's a skill
          that will serve you a hell of a lot more
          than anything you learned at Brown!

CHIP, the intern, dashes in with the car keys, all smiles.

                    INTERN
          Here you go, washed and detailed. I even
          had them put one of those lemon air
          fresheners in the little can under the
          front seat.

MS Katz snatches up her purse, grabs the keys, and heads for
the door.

                    MS KATZ
          Whad'ya want Biff, a cookie?

                         CHIP
          Ah...

She moves past him out the door, completely ignoring him.

                         CHIP (cont'd)
          ...it's Chip.
                (to the Assistant)
          Is it me or is she kind of a bitch?

                         ASSISTANT
          It's you.

MS Katz comes back into the room.

                         MS KATZ
          Um-hum, excuse me princess... are you
          coming?

The Assistant is clueless.

                         MS KATZ (CONT'D)
          Listen to me, pull your head out of your
          ass and start using it, then get tough
          and you might be around a while. Stay
          the nice, STUPID girl that you are and
          you'll get killed in this town.

MS Katz walks away.

                         MS KATZ (cont'd)
          It's your choice... I wish you would make
          it soon... I'm tired of wasting my time
          on you.

The assistant follows her out the door.

INT. CAR - NIGHT (MOVING) - LATER

The Assistant is driving MS Katz's Mercedes.

                         MS KATZ
          I loath these damn award dinners!

                         ASSISTANT
          Then why are we going?

                         MS KATZ
          I'm going because they are giving ME the
          Humanitarian of the Year award and you're
          going because I've gotta get loaded just
          to sit at the same table as these putzes.
                (pointing)
          Pull up over there.

                    ASSISTANT
          Why don't we just valet it?

                    MS KATZ
          You're not going in.

The Assistant stares blankly.

                    MS KATZ (cont'd)
          You're here to drive me home.

                    ASSISTANT
          I can join you without drinking. I have
          self-control.

                    MS KATZ
          Yeah, well that's not your job. This is.

MS Katz hands her assistant a piece of paper.

                    MS KATZ (cont'd)
          I made of list of things I need you to
          do. You should have plenty of time, I
          don't anticipate leaving until after
          eleven, but whatever you do, don't be
          late picking me up.

EXT. DARK STREET IN BAD NEIGHBORHOOD - LATER

The car sputters to a stop beneath a street lamp on the
desolate street. A bum stumbles by. It's dark. Spooky.
This is not a good place to be stranded. Ever.

INT. MERCEDES (PARKED) - CONTINUOUS

The Assistant cranks it a couple of times to no avail.

                    THE ASSISTANT
          Shhht... this can't be happening... c'mon
          start.

She tries to start it again then looks at the dash. The gas
gage reads empty.

                    THE ASSISTANT (CONT'D)
          Son of a... the little turd washes it,
          details it... puts a stinking air thingy
          in it...

She picks up the freshener and throws it out the window.

                    THE ASSISTANT (cont'd)
          ...but doesn't buy a drop of gas! He _is_
          an idiot!

She mumbles while dialing her phone. Ring, Ring. She looks
out the window.

BANG! Startled, she flings the phone across the car.

She scrambles to pick it up. Listens. Nothing but static.
She mutters while punching in a number. More static. On
closer inspection, she sees the phone is broken.

> THE ASSISTANT (cont'd)
> Why did I buy a crap Google phone!

EXT. CAR (PARKED) - CONTINUOUS

The car is engulfed in dark nothingness... a scary kind of
nothing filled with noises and moving objects.

Inside the car, she throws the phone down in frustration,
takes a deep breath and surveys her surroundings...

INT. CAR (PARKED) - CONTINUOUS

...and assess the situation.

> THE ASSISTANT
> Mental note... castrate Chip to keep him
> from reproducing.
>   (deep breath)
> So, what are my options? I could sit
> here until someone comes by...

Sounds of a scuffle draw her attention. She looks out the
window to see a BUM and BAG LADY involved in a brutal
fistfight over what appears to be an empty plastic bottle.

> THE ASSISTANT (cont'd)
> There's got to be a movie in that.
>   (thinking)
> I could walk, but I'm a little safer in a
> locked car, I think.

She presses the lock button. Out of the corner of her eye,
she sees a PAYPHONE. It's about half a block away,
illuminated by a dim light inside the booth.

> THE ASSISTANT (cont'd)
> Bingo. Survive trip to the payphone.
> Call Triple A. Survive trip back to the
> car. Wait for gas to arrive.

She takes another good look outside the car. Nothing...
except the darkness, which is scary.

                    THE ASSISTANT (cont'd)
          Damn! I've seen this movie... it never
          ends well.

EXT. CAR - CONTINUOUS

She steps out, uneasy, still talking to herself.

                    THE ASSISTANT
          The woman always gets raped and murdered.

She slams the car door shut.

                    THE ASSISTANT (cont'd)
          I just hope they're cute.

She clicks her remote, locking the doors.

INSERT SHOT: CLOSE-UP OF DOOR LOCK LOCKING

She takes two steps then stops.

                    THE ASSISTANT
          Wait a minute. What if I need to get
          back in the car quickly. In the movies,
          the girl always gets killed trying to
          unlock the car door.

She clicks the remote again.

INSERT SHOT: CLOSE-UP OF DOOR LOCK UNLOCKING

She takes a few more steps then stops again.

                    THE ASSISTANT
          In the movies, they don't have remote
          door locks, stupid. Let alone an
          expensive stereo system with a ten disc
          CD changer that belongs to a super bitch.

She clicks the remote again.

INSERT: CLOSE-UP OF DOOR LOCK LOCKING.

She takes three more steps.

                    THE ASSISTANT
          Then again, what if I'm running back to
          the car and I drop the remote. They
          always do that in those movies.
                    (beat)
          Screw the Bitch.

INSERT: CLOSE-UP OF DOOR LOCK UNLOCKING

EXT. PHONE BOOTH - CONTINUOUS

The Assistant approaches the dimly lit booth swiftly.

INT. PHONE BOOTH - CONTINUOUS

She enters frantically digging in her purse for a quarter.
Looking side to side and cursing, she grabs the receiver and
puts a quarter into the phone. Six rings later...

INT.   TRIPLE-A OFFICE - CONTINUOUS

The TRIPLE-A GUY finally picks up.

>   TRIPLE-A GUY
>   Triple-A...

INT. PHONE BOOTH - CONTINUOUS

Crosscut phone conversation.

>   THE ASSISTANT
>   I need gas.

>   TRIPLE-A GUY
>   Try baked beans. They always give me
>   gas.

>   THE ASSISTANT
>   Is this Triple-A or Morons-R-Us?!

>   TRIPLE-A GUY
>   If I'm the moron, how come you're calling
>   me for gas?

>   THE ASSISTANT
>   Because God's an angry little man,
>   Goober. Now get off your ass and bring
>   me some gas, pronto!

She looks at the car. It's eerie. Silent.

>   THE ASSISTANT (cont'd)
>   How long will it be? This is not exactly
>   Mister Rogers' Neighborhood.

>   TRIPLE-A GUY
>   About an hour.

>   THE ASSISTANT
>   An hour?!

>   TRIPLE-A GUY
>   Just lock yourself in your car and don't
>   draw any attention to yourself.

                    THE ASSISTANT
          Oh, darn, I was gonna dance naked on the
          roof until you got here!

She slams down the receiver.

INT. TRIPLE-A OFFICE - CONTINUOUS

The Triple-A guy winces.

                    TRIPLE-A GUY
          Geez, what a bitch!

EXT. STREET

The Assistant moves lickety-split, looking in every
direction, hastily stepping through the darkness faster and
faster until she's running full tilt.

She hits the driver's door, opens it, and quickly slides in.

INT. CAR

She slams the door, locks it, and sighs in relief. She
remembers the stereo. Checks it. It's there. She sighs
again, then leans back into the seat.

Movement startles her.

WIDER

A LITTLE OLD LADY is in the passenger seat. They scream.

     THE ASSISTANT   LITTLE OLD LADY
Ahhhhhhggg...!   Ahhhhggggg!

They look at each other and scream again.

     THE ASSISTANT   LITTLE OLD LADY (cont'd)
Ahhhggggg!   Ahhhggggg!

                    THE ASSISTANT
          Who the hell are you and what the fuck
          are you doing in my car?

                    LITTLE OLD LADY
          I'm... uh, I..., well I--

                    THE ASSISTANT
          Never mind, never mind... it doesn't
          matter! Just get out! Get out!

The Little Old Lady struggles to breathe.

                    THE ASSISTANT (cont'd)
Do not pass out `cause I'm not giving you
mouth to mouth!

                    LITTLE OLD LADY
My good Lord, you gave me quite a start,
young lady.

                    THE ASSISTANT
You're the one in my car! You scared the
shit out of me, lady!

                    OLD LADY
I missed my bus.

                    THE ASSISTANT
Get an Uber!

                    OLD LADY
I was on my way home from the senior
center where I play bingo. Well, things
went a little late this evening because
Herb Schulman was calling the numbers and
between his stuttering and my Alzheimer's
things got a little confusing.

                    THE ASSISTANT
What are you yammering about?

                    LITTLE OLD LADY
I would have called a cab, but I'm on a
fixed income, you know, so I have to
watch my money.

                    THE ASSISTANT
Here's five dollars. Call a cab.

                    LITTLE OLD LADY
Oh, no, those cab drivers don't ever
speak English, most of them smell funny,
and they take you miles out of the way
just to run up the meter. Why, one time,
I think it must have been oh, back in `67
I think it was...

                    THE ASSISTANT
I thought you had Alzheimer's? Stop
talking and GET out.

                    LITTLE OLD LADY
It's only a few blocks. I'd walk, but I
don't walk so good anymore... I remember
when I was a girl, I walked everywhere.
Why, one time Clara Mae Johnson and I
walked all the way from--

                    THE ASSISTANT
                 (cutting her off)
          Hey, earth to little old lady, work with
          me here.

She feigns sign language.

                    THE ASSISTANT (cont'd)
          Why... are you... in my car?

                    LITTLE OLD LADY
          Well, I was coming to that young lady
          there's no need to be rude.

                    THE ASSISTANT
          Just answer the question!

                    LITTLE OLD LADY
          I was being stalked.

                    THE ASSISTANT
          Stalked?

                    LITTLE OLD LADY
          Yes! There was a man--

                    THE ASSISTANT
          So, you said to yourself, rather than die
          alone, I'll get a complete stranger
          killed, too?!

The Assistant spins around searching the area for a would-be
attacker... nothing to the left, nothing to the right.

                    LITTLE OLD LADY
          No. Huh? What?

The Assistant pushes her toward the door.

                    THE ASSISTANT
          You heard me, out!

                    LITTLE OLD LADY
          You can't be serious. What if there's
          someone out there.

                    THE ASSISTANT
          Jab with your left! Now go.

Splat! Something hits the windshield.

     THE ASSISTANT (cont'd)   LITTLE OLD LADY
Aaahhhh!!!   Aaahhh!!!

A blob of wet newspaper moves across the windshield to reveal
a BUM using it. The Assistant rolls down her window.

                    THE ASSISTANT
          Stop that right now!

                    BUM
          Clean your windows lady?

                    THE ASSISTANT
          NO! The car was just washed. Go away!

                    LITTLE OLD LADY
          You shouldn't antagonize them. Just give
          him a dollar and he'll go away.

                    THE ASSISTANT
          I'm not giving him a dollar. And please
          feel free to join him. You'll be safe.
          There's two of you now.
              (to the bum)
          NO! Don't touch my window! No, no, no!

The bum presses his filthy face against the window.

                    BUM
          Clean it up real good for you lady.

He spits on it.

                    THE ASSISTANT
          Stop, you filthy bastard!

                    LITTLE OLD LADY
          My, you're a mean one.

                    THE ASSISTANT
          Nobody asked you, lady?

The Bum comes around to the Old Lady's side of the car and
taps on her window. The Old Lady rummages through her purse
and pulls out a dollar bill, then gives to the bum.

                    BUM
          Thanks, lady.
              (glaring at the assistant)
          No offense, but your granddaughter is a
          real bitch.

                    OLD LADY
          Oh, we're not related.
              (whispering)
          But she is a little bitchy.

                    THE ASSISTANT
          Screw you both.

The Bum walks away.

                    LITTLE OLD LADY
          Now, why couldn't you give that poor man
          a dollar for goodness sake? What kind of
          person are you?

                    THE ASSISTANT
          You're nuts? You can't go around handing
          out money to bums in alleys. Or picking
          up strange old ladies in the middle of
          L.A., for that matter. Do you know what
          that'll get you?

                    OLD LADY
          A warm fuzzy feeling.

                    THE ASSISTANT
          Dead! Dead is what it'll get you.

                    OLD LADY
          Helping a stranger get something to eat,
          or an old woman get home isn't going to
          kill you. It's the decent thing to do.
          But you wouldn't know that because you
          are a--

                    THE ASSISTANT
          A what?

                    OLD LADY
          Nothing.

                    THE ASSISTANT
          No, no. Say it. A what?

                    OLD LADY
          I was always taught that if you can't say
          anything nice you shouldn't say anything
          at all. So, I'll just get my things
          together and be on my way.

                    THE ASSISTANT
          Good!

The old lady gathers up her things. The Assistant feels a
twinge of guilt.

                    THE ASSISTANT (CONT'D)
          Okay, that was a little harsh. Maybe it
          would be wrong to put an old lady out in
          the middle of a neighborhood like this.

                    THE ASSISTANT (CONT'D)
              (beat to consider the idea)
          But I don't like you. So, keep packing
          and get outta my car!

                    OLD LADY
          My word! If your grandmother is ever
          stranded in a situation like this, I hope
          she runs into a much nicer person than
          you.

                    THE ASSISTANT
          You don't know anything about my
          grandmother.

                    LITTLE OLD LADY
          I know she has a flaming bitch for a
          granddaughter.

The old lady struggles to open the door.

                    THE ASSISTANT
          Damn it! Okay... you can stay. But only
          until the Triple-A guy gets here.

                    LITTLE OLD LADY
          I was hoping you'd take me back to my
          house... it's getting late and I haven't
          had my medication. It's really not very
          far.

The Assistant thinks about her grandmother.

                    THE ASSISTANT
          Alright, alright, I'll take you home!

                    LITTLE OLD LADY
          There now. Don't you feel good? It's so
          much better to be nice.

                    THE ASSISTANT
          I suppose. It's just that, I'm in a
          tough business, you know, and being nice
          is a sign of weakness. If you're nice
          they'll eat you alive. You know what I
          mean?

                    LITTLE OLD LADY
          Oh yes. I've been there.

Flashing lights in the rearview mirror.

                    THE ASSISTANT
          Please let that be Triple-A.

The assistant sees a reflection of someone exiting a vehicle
in the rearview mirror.

There is a tap on the window. The Assistant lowers it.

                    THE ASSISTANT (CONT'D)
          The gas tank is on the other side.

EXT. CAR - CONTINUOUS

A MALE POLICE OFFICER leans over to look into her window. A
FEMALE OFFICER walks up to the passenger window.

                    MALE OFFICER
          Please lower the window all the way,
          ma'am.

The Assistant complies.

                    THE ASSISTANT
          I'm sorry officer. I thought you were
          the auto club people.

                    MALE OFFICER
          What seems to be the problem?

                    THE ASSISTANT
          I ran out of gas, but I called Triple A.
          This woman missed her bus. I was going
          to give her a ride, but since you guys
          are here, I really have to pick up my
          boss or she'll kill me.

                    FEMALE OFFICER
          This is not a great neighborhood to run
          out of gas in.

                    MALE OFFICER
          Or for picking up strangers.
               (smiling at the old lady)
          Even if they are little old ladies.

The old lady keeps her head down.

                    THE ASSISTANT
          What are ya gonna do? You have to try
          and be a decent person, right?

                    FEMALE OFFICER
          That's very nice of you. I tell you
          what... why don't I take this lady home
          and my partner will wait here with you
          until the gas arrives.

                    THE ASSISTANT
          Thank you.

                    LITTLE OLD LADY
          Oh, no, no, no. That won't be necessary.
          She'll take me... she's a very nice girl.

                    FEMALE OFFICER
          It's no problem, ma'am.

                    THE ASSISTANT
               (to the old lady)
          I think that's best. That way we both
          have a police escort.

The Female Officer opens the passenger door. The old lady
pulls it shut.

                    LITTLE OLD LADY
          I prefer to have <u>this</u> nice young lady
          take me home.

                    FEMALE OFFICER
          It's okay, grandma. I'm a nice lady
          myself... you'll get home quick and safe.
          I'm might even turn on the siren for you.

                    LITTLE OLD LADY
               (sharply)
          Shove your siren, fuzz.

The female officer pulls the door, but the unusually strong
old lady keeps it shut.

                    THE ASSISTANT
          Lady, she's going to take you home.

                    LITTLE OLD LADY
          Didn't you learn anything from our little
          talk, deary?

                    THE ASSISTANT
          Hey, I was nice! I was going to take you
          home, but now I don't need to. So, go
          with the cop.

                    LITTLE OLD LADY
          No. I want you.

                    FEMALE OFFICER
          Look, lady, she doesn't want to take you
          home. So, just get out of the car and
          I'll take your old ass home.

The Female Officer yanks open the door and grabs the old lady
by the arm.

                    LITTLE OLD LADY
          No! No! No!

                    OFFICER #2
          Calm down, ma'am.
              (to The Assistant)
          Has she shown any signs of senility?

                    LITTLE OLD LADY
          Screw you, pig! I'm not senile.

The Assistant laughs. The Male Officer rushes to the other
side of the car.

                    MALE OFFICER
          That's enough!

The Female Officer yanks the old lady's arm.

                    THE ASSISTANT
          Hey, don't hurt her. She's like a
          hundred years old!

                    MALE OFFICER
          Stay there, ma'am. Nobody is getting
          hurt.

The old lady grabs a huge meat cleaver out of her bag and
chops the Female Officer in the groin.

Blood spews from her leg. She screams and stumbles back from
the open car door.

The Assistant screams. The old lady swings the cleaver at
her.

The Male Officer cranks three rounds into the old lady's
back. The impact knocks the old lady on top of the
Assistant, who is screaming hysterically.

The Male Officer rushes to his partner.

INT. CAR - CONTINUOUS

The old lady pushes herself up. A gray wig drops in the
Assistant's lap. She screams!

The old lady is a small man holding a cleaver. He grabs the
Assistant by the throat and pins her against the door.

He raises the cleaver to kill her, but she holds back his
arm.

>   THE ASSISTANT
>   You're bleeding on my boss' leather
>   seats, bitch!

She kicks him out of the passenger door.

EXT. CAR - CONTINUOUS

He lands at the feet of the cops.

The Female Officer empties her clip into him as he continues swinging his cleaver at her.

The Assistant thinks about her boss's advice.

>   MS KATZ (V.O.)
>   Stay the nice, STUPID girl that you are
>   and you'll get killed in this town.

EXT. CAR - PARKED - LATER

Flashing lights reflect in the windows as OTHER COPS and PARAMEDICS tend to their business.

The Assistant sits in the police car with the Male Officer.

>   THE ASSISTANT
>   He sure fooled me.

>   MALE OFFICER
>   He fooled a lot of people. He's the
>   serial killer we've been looking for.

>   THE ASSISTANT
>   This guy is a serial killer?!

>   MALE OFFICER
>   Yeah, his female victims were raped and
>   chopped into little pieces. The "Little
>   Old Lady" scam is why we could never
>   catch him, I guess. We were looking for
>   a man.

>   THE ASSISTANT
>   So, by being nice and taking the old hag
>   home, I was going to be raped and
>   murdered?

>   MALE OFFICER
>   Oh yeah, you were dead. And eaten. Did
>   I mention he ate parts of his victims?

The assistant fires up one of her boss's cigarettes, leans back, and exhales.

                    THE ASSISTANT
          Screw this! The Bitch was right! I'll
          never be nice again!

INT. KAPPA ALPHA PSI - LATER

Myth Mistress holds up her SMOVE steady-cam stick for a wide
view of the party while finishing off another Bud Light,
clearly feeling the cumulative effect.

                    MYTH MISTRESS
          Interesting variation of the old, "don't
          give rides to strangers" myth!
               (beat)
          That was a great story, and while the
          danger of becoming a victim is always
          real, it's nowhere near what this myth
          makes it out to be. Geez, I hope you
          didn't buy into that one! But...
               (she shows the party)
          Look, I'm at the Kappa Alpha Psi party...
          if you're not here, get here, and if you
          are here... come say hi! Don't let the
          serial killer prediction scare ya...
          Hell, there may be one here... who
          knows... what do you think?

TERRY comes up to the Myth Mistress.

                    MYTH MISTRESS (cont'd)
          Hey, Ter-bear! 'Sup?
               (into the camera)
          Everybody, this is my good friend, Terry.
          Terry this is everybody. All...

She looks at the counter that reads 500,000 viewers.

                    MYTH MISTRESS (cont'd)
          Five hundred sixty-two thousand of them!
          Woop Woop! A Myth Mistress's work is
          never done.
               (finishes her beer)
          But at least it's a workin' party!

Myth Mistress grabs another Bud Light.

                    TERRY
          Did you hear? Dan's dead.

                    MYTH MISTRESS
          Dan got me once tonight. No way I'm
          falling for it again.

                    TERRY
          Seriously, Dan's dead. I just spoke to
          Campus Police. It was not too far from
          here.

                    MYTH MISTRESS
          Nope. Not gonna get me... that's not
          even possible... I just left him a few
          minutes ago.

                    TERRY
          Guess you're lucky then... it could have
          been you.

                    MYTH MISTRESS
          Hmmm... Do they know who killed him?

                    TERRY
          My guess...

                    MYTH MISTRESS
          Don't even say it!

                    TERRY
          Little Bo Peep.

                    MYTH MISTRESS
          Fuckin' Milly!

Member's live comments stream across her iPhone screen.

**INSERT: THERE'S A KILLER ON CAMPUS?! IS THIS A JOKE? THE
PREDICTION SAID "MASS MURDER" SO MORE TO COME?!**

                    MYTH MISTRESS
          No, no, don't jump to conclusions,
          everybody! Settle down, we'll find out
          what happened together.

She takes off a bit tipsy.

                    MYTH MISTRESS (cont'd)
          Whoa... that free beer went to my head...
               (stumbling)
          Or my heels...

Terry grabs her arm to steady her as they go out the door.

EXT. CAMPUS - NIGHT - CONTINUOUS

Terry and Myth Mistress come out the door heading across the
lawn toward the area where a crowd has gathered.

She turns the phone to show her audience the scene.

Police tape cordons off a large area. COPS question
Halloween costumed STUDENTS. Many of them dressed as Little
Bo Peep.

>   MYTH MISTRESS
>   It looks like my friend, Dan, really was
>   killed.

The live comments stream across her screen.

INSERT: WTF! OMG! THERE'S A KILLER ON CAMPUS?! MASS
MURDERER MEANS MORE DEATHS TO COME?!

>   MYTH MISTRESS
>   Stop it, people! Don't jump to
>   conclusions about Milly's mass murderer
>   bullshit! Let me clear my head.

INSERT: I KILLED YOUR FRIEND. I'LL KILL YOU TOO. BUT NOT
UNTIL MIDNIGHT. UNTIL THEN THERE WILL BE OTHERS.

>   MYTH MISTRESS
>   WTF people! Who's the sicko?

INSERT: I'M GOING TO KILL YOU AT MIDNIGHT! I'M GOING TO
KILL YOU AT MIDNIGHT! I'M GOING TO KILL YOU AT MIDNIGHT!
I'M GOING TO KILL YOU AT MIDNIGHT! I'M GOING TO KILL YOU AT
MIDNIGHT! I'M GOING TO KILL YOU AT MIDNIGHT! I'M GOING TO
KILL YOU!

More comments stream.

INSERT: OMG! YOU'RE DEAD. RUN. HIDE. SOMEONE THREATENED
TO KILL YOU, MM? WTF!! IT IS A SERIAL KILLER!

>   MYTH MISTRESS
>   Don't worry. Someone is just being a
>   doucebag. Nobody write anything. I have
>   a question for the asshole that killed
>   Dan! Why did you kill my friend?

INSERT: I KILLED YOUR FRIEND BECAUSE I SAW HIM WITH YOU.
NOBODY GETS YOU... BUT ME.

>   MYTH MISTRESS
>   You saw us?

INSERT: I WAS RIGHT BEHIND YOU. WATCHING. I'M STILL
WATCHING. AM I BEHIND YOU NOW?

>   MYTH MISTRESS
>   You didn't kill anybody. You're just a
>   prick trying to scare me.

Slightly concerned, she scans the area. Little Bo Peeps are all around her, but the cops are gone.

INSERT: GET OUT OF THERE! GO FIND THE COPS! RUN! HIDE! LOCK YOURSELF UP! THE PSYCHIC PREDICTED THIS WOULD HAPPEN.

                    MYTH MISTRESS
          Whoever is doing this please stop!! This
          is not funny. It's not the psychic's
          prediction, it's just some deranged idiot
          acting out because of it.

INSERT: HOW CAN YOU SAY THAT? WHO DO YOU THINK YOU ARE? I KILLED DAN. I WILL KILL MORE… THEN I WILL KILL YOU.

                    MYTH MISTRESS
          WHY?!

INSERT: BECAUSE YOU BELONG TO ME. WE BELONG TOGETHER!

                    MYTH MISTRESS (cont'd)
          No, we don't, you sick fuck!

INSERT: THE PSYCHIC WAS RIGHT. LITTLE BO PEEP IS COMING FOR YOU ALL. ESPECIALLY YOU, KIM. AT MIDNIGHT YOU DIE.

                    MYTH MISTRESS
          How do you know my name?

INSERT: I KNOW YOU. YOU KNOW ME. YOU'RE NEXT. MAYBE. I'LL PROBABLY KILL SOME MORE ON MY WAY TO YOU. UNLESS I SEE YOU FIRST.

                    MYTH MISTRESS
          It's already midnight, dumbass. Too,
          late!

INSERT: I'M RIGHT BEHIND YOU.

Myth Mistress spins around.

Many LITTLE BO PEEPS come at her.

                    ONE LITTLE BO PEEP
          Hey, Myth Mistress!

She runs. WHAM! Knocked on her ass by a huge DUDE. He reaches for her. She screams. Then kicks him in the nuts and bolts away zigzagging between dimly lit patches of campus and the BO PEEPS as fast as she can.

She stops under a light to catch her breath and speak to the viewers.

                    MYTH MISTRESS
          One of you call campus police! Everyone
          else watch this video. I'll try to make
          it back to the bunker.

She clicks on the next video. A WOMAN talks into her phone.

                    WOMAN
          This really happened to my aunt's second
          husband's brother's dad.

                    MYTH MISTRESS
          Stop with the who told whom! I swear,
          people! Just say I heard this!! Damn
          it! It's never a first-hand account!
          But it's okay to tell us that.

                                        CUT TO THE MYTH:

EXT. STREET - DAY

DR. JACKSON, African American (50s), gets into an Uber.

INT. UBER CAR - CONTINUOUS

The driver continues down the road.

                    DRIVER
          Sparta, huh? That's a long drive.

                    DR. JACKSON
          I need to get there and back by morning.

                    DRIVER
          Sparta and back in one night? Why?

                    DR. JACKSON
          There was an unusual death. The local
          doctor determined the death was a heart
          attack, but the girl was so young. So,
          they requested I come take a look.

                    DRIVER
          You suspect foul play or something?

                    DR. JACKSON
          Most times there are simple explanations
          for death. If you know how to ask the
          dead the right questions, they will tell
          you many things.

                    DRIVER
          You speak to the dead?

                    DR. JACKSON
          They speak to me.
               (off the driver's look)
          I'm a Forensic Pathologist.

EXT. SPARTA - MORGUE - LATE AFTERNOON

The car pulls up to the building.

                    DR. JACKSON
          It shouldn't take more than two hours.

                    DRIVER
          I'll be at the local greasy spoon.

INT. THE MORGUE - MOMENTS LATER

Dr. Jackson enters and approaches the female ATTENDANT on
duty.

                    DR. JACKSON
          Excuse me, I'm Dr. Henry Jackson. I'm
          here to examine the young girl that died
          of cardiac arrest.

                    ATTENDANT
          Right, this way.

The Attendant escorts the doctor to the lab.

                    ATTENDANT (cont'd)
          I'll be down the hall if you need
          anything.

                    DR. JACKSON
          Thank you.

Dr. Jackson heads toward a large FEMALE BODY on the table in
the middle of the room as we...

                                        DISSOLVE TO:

EXT. THE MORGUE - TWO HOURS LATER

It's raining as Dr. Jackson exits the building and steps into
the car.

                    DRIVER
          What's the verdict, doc?

                    DR. JACKSON
          It was unusual, but she died from cardiac
          arrest. She had a history of smoking K2.

                    DRIVER
          K2?

                    DR. JACKSON
          Synthetic marijuana.

                    DRIVER
          She told you that?

                    DR. JACKSON
          Her body did. Confirmed by her medical
          records.

                    DRIVER
          Smoking K2 can kill you?

                    DR. JACKSON
          Yes. Several teenagers in Texas died
          from cardiac arrest after smoking it just
          once.

                    DRIVER
          Well, you just never know, do ya Doc?

The car drives away.

                                        DISSOLVE TO:

INT. CAB - (MOVING) - LATER THAT NIGHT

Rain pounds the cab unmercifully. The road is a dark watery
blur through the windshield.

                    DRIVER
          What the hell is that?

The two men struggle to see through the downpour.

                    DR. JACKSON
          It's a person! Stop!

EXT. SIDE OF THE ROAD - CONTINUOUS

The car screeches to a halt before hitting a large drenched
WOMAN standing motionless in the middle of the road.

INT. CAB - CONTINUOUS

                    DRIVER
          Why would anyone be out here in the
          middle of nowhere, in this rain, at this
          time of night?

                    DR. JACKSON
          We must give her a ride.

                         DRIVER
              No, Doc. It's against policy to pick up
              hitchhikers. Can't do it!

EXT. SIDE OF THE ROAD - CONTINUOUS

Dr. Jackson pokes his head out of the window.

                         DR. JACKSON
              Do you need a ride, miss?

The woman remains motionless. Dr. Jackson sticks his head
further out the window.

                         DR. JACKSON (cont'd)
              Are you all right? Do you need help?

She doesn't speak.

                         DR. JACKSON (cont'd)
              Please, come inside the car.

The driver is perturbed as the woman moves slowly, silently,
into the cab.

INT. CAB - CONTINUOUS

She glides into the back seat, expressionless, extremely
pale, soaked from the rain, but does not demonstrate any
symptoms of being cold. The driver proceeds down the road.

                         DRIVER
              What the hell, lady! Why were you
              standing in the middle of the road in
              this downpour?! You're lucky we didn't
              run you over!

She says nothing. She doesn't move. Doesn't blink. It's
creepy.

                         DR. JACKSON
              Are you all right, miss?

No response. No reaction whatsoever.

                         DRIVER
              She's crazy, Doc. Out here. In this.
              Soaking wet. Not saying a word.

She doesn't move. There is no change in her demeanor.

                         DRIVER (cont'd)
              It's creepy.

   Doctor Lee stares at her.

                    DR. JACKSON
          Have we met before?

The woman slowly turns her head and stares at Dr. Jackson.

EXT. OUT IN THE MIDDLE OF NOWHERE - CONTINUOUS

The car disappears into the rainy darkness...

EXT. OUT IN THE MIDDLE OF NOWHERE - LATER

Cutting across the countryside...

EXT. OUT IN THE MIDDLE OF NOWHERE - HOURS LATER

Speeding through the rainy night, seemingly forever.

INT. CAB - CONTINUOUS

The driver wipes the foggy windshield, mumbling. The women's expression has not changed. She has not spoken or moved and is still drenched after all the hours of driving.

                    DR. JACKSON
               (to the woman)
          Don't worry, we're not lost.

                    DRIVER
          I'm glad you're so sure. We've been
          driving for hours and I don't see
          nothing.

                    DR. JACKSON
          Are you sure you're okay?

No reaction from the woman.

                    DR. JACKSON (cont'd)
               (quietly to the driver)
          I've seen this woman somewhere before, I
          believe.

                    WOMAN
          Let me out.

                    DRIVER
          It speaks!

                    DR. JACKSON
          You can't get out here...

                    DRIVER
          Yes, she can! She gives me the heebie-
          jeebies. Let her out! Let her out!

The driver slams on the break.

> DR. JACKSON
> We are lost in the middle of nowhere!

> DRIVER
> We're not lost!! You said so yourself!
> I've been driving for hours and we're
> still in the middle of nowhere. She's
> the reason. I want her out!

The woman gets out of the car. The driver floors it.

Dr. Jackson looks back to check on her. She's gone.

> DR. JACKSON
> She disappeared. Stop!

The driver slams on the brakes again.

> DRIVER
> What?! Why?

> DR. JACKSON
> Back up.

> DRIVER
> No way! We're getting as far away from
> her as possible!

> DR. JACKSON
> She looked different somehow, but I think
> that's the woman I examined. I need to
> return to Sparta.

> DRIVER
> What the hell, doc! You think she's a
> ghost and you want to go back! Screw
> that.

> DR. JACKSON
> I have you until morning. Turn around!

INT. MORGUE - LATER

Dr. Jackson rushes over to the covered body and pulls back
the sheet. It's the same woman from the car.

> DR. JACKSON
> What in the hell...

BANG! Dr, Jackson looks over at an EMT smashing a gurney
through the double doors.

                    EMT
          Dr. Jackson? Why are you here?

                    DR. JACKSON
          I came back to reexamine the body.

                    EMT
          Came back? Wait, what body?

                    DR. JACKSON
          This body.

Dr. Jackson looks down. The woman is gone.

                    EMT
          The only body we've had is this one.

He uncovers the body revealing the same woman.

                    DR. JACKSON
          Impossible. I examined that body hours
          ago. Then I picked her up on the road
          back to St. Louis. She demanded to be
          let out and then she vanished. So, I
          came back to take another look at her
          corpse.

                    EMT
          You been drinking? Cause that's freakin'
          insane. We JUST picked up this body.
          Think about what you're saying.

                    DR. JACKSON
          I haven't been drinking. It happened.
          Never mind about how it sounds. I'm not
          crazy. Put her on the examination table.
          Something's not right.

                    EMT
          I'll say.

EXT. MORGUE - SUNRISE

Dr. Jackson exits the morgue and gets into the waiting Uber.

                    DRIVER
          So, what happened?

                    DR. JACKSON
          She was murdered.

EXT. VICTIM'S HOUSE - FRONT PORCH - SAME TIME

Two SHERIFF DEPUTIES handcuff the HUSBAND.

                    DR. JACKSON (V.O.)
          Her husband is being arrested as we
          speak.

BACK INSIDE THE UBER

                    DRIVER
          What?! How was a murder mistaken for a
          heart attack?

                    DR. JACKSON
          Hyperkalemia. Her husband gave her a
          shot that contained a very high potassium
          content.

INT. VICTIM'S HOUSE - BEDROOM - EARLIER THAT DAY

The dead woman is passed out on the sofa. Her husband
injects her between the toes.

                    DR. JACKSON (V.O.)
          The puncture mark between her toes was
          overlooked due to her history of drug
          use.

BACK INSIDE THE UBER

                    DRIVER
          Potassium? Like in bananas? How does
          that kill you?

                    DR. JACKSON
          Cardiac arrest.

                    DRIVER
          Potassium gave her a heart attack?!
          Wouldn't that show up or something?

                    DR. JACKSON
          Her being young did raise suspicions.
          But heart attacks are fairly common,
          especially for at-risk patients.
                    (beat)
          She was an obese drug user. The original
          autopsy found the heart attack - so
          there's your cause of death. The heart
          attack via hyperkalemia was mistaken as a
          coronary blockage instead.

                    DRIVER
          So, she did speak to you.

> DR. JACKSON
> She spoke to us both. She's the one that
> kept us from leaving the area. I'm
> certain of it now.

> DRIVER
> That's creepy! I knew something was
> wrong with her! How is that even
> possible?

> DR. JACKSON
> It's inconceivable. She was dead. Yet,
> her spirit somehow reached out through
> time and space and stopped us. When I
> returned she was there on the table.
> Then they wheeled her body in and when I
> looked down she was no longer on my
> table.

> DRIVER
> Holy shit!

> DR. JACKSON
> She kept me from making a huge mistake
> and put the blame where it belonged.
> Now she can rest in peace.

> DRIVER
> Now can we get the hell outta here?!

EXT. MYTH MISTRESS'S DORM - LATER

Myth Mistress, her back against the wall by the door,
breathing heavily, searches the area for movement.

> MYTH MISTRESS
> I'm not going to lie...

She cautiously opens the door peering down a long dark
corridor.

> MYTH MISTRESS (cont'd)
> This is scary, guys.

INT. DORM - CONTINUOUS

She enters.

> BO PEEP (O.C.)
> AAAAHHHH!!!

BO PEEP jumps out of the shadows. She screams, throwing
herself back against the door, scared as hell!

                    BO PEEP (cont'd)
               (laughing)
     I thought you liked being scared.

She pushes him aside, rushing to the elevator. DING. She
freezes! It's empty. She enters, presses the floor button,
and looks up. ANOTHER BO PEEP stares back at her.

                    MYTH MISTRESS
     What the fuck, people!!

Bo Peep bum rushes her, knocking her to the ground.

                    MYTH MISTRESS (cont'd)
     Get away from me!

                    ANOTHER BO PEEP
     I'll get you, bitch!

Myth Mistress runs out of the elevator into the stairwell and
up the stairs, screaming all the way to the third-floor door.

Stopping behind it, she opens it slightly to confirm the
coast is clear. She moves quickly to her room crashing
through the door! Right into LITTLE BO PEEP!

                    MILLY
     What the fuck, Kim!

                    MYTH MISTRESS
     Damn it, Milly, you scared the shit out
     of me! Again!

                    MILLY
     I thought you liked being scared
     shitless.

                    MYTH MISTRESS
     Fuck! Will everyone stop saying that!

                    MILLY
     Not so tough when it actually happens,
     huh?
               (beat)
     Pyscho...

Myth Mistress ignores her, moving quickly to the myth bunker
and activating all the equipment.

All camera views pop on screen.

Milly stands behind her in the doorway texting. A scowl on
her face.

A message pops on screen.

INSERT: YOU'RE NOT SAFE YET.

> MYTH MISTRESS
> I thought you were going to kill me at
> midnight!

INSERT: I AM.

> MYTH MISTRESS
> Face it. This is all an urban legend and
> you're some maniacal meathead who killed
> my friend. Not some prophesied serial
> killer.

**INSERT: I KILLED YOUR FRIEND. I KILLED OTHERS. AND I WILL
KILL YOU AT MIDNIGHT. I AM THE LITTLE BO PEEP KILLER!**

> MYTH MISTRESS
> You-are-a-nimrod! Besides, it's past
> midnight, doofus.

INSERT: I NEVER SAID WHAT TIME ZONE.

> MYTH MISTRESS
> Time zone?
>   (beat)
> You're full of shit, asshole!

INSERT: AM I? LOOK BEHIND YOU.

Myth Mistress spins around. Milly is still texting.

> MYTH MISTRESS
> Milly, are you doing this?

> MILLY
>   (looking up)
> Doing what?

> MYTH MISTRESS
> Threatening me!

Myth Mistress jumps up grabbing Milly with both hands.

> MILLY
> Let go of me, you loud mouth bitch!

Milly pushes her away.

> MILLY (cont'd)
> I hate you! You and your dumb website.
> You think you're so cool dressed in your
> slutty outfit strutting all over campus
> acting like you're all mysterious, but
> you _want_ everyone to know who you are.

                    MILLY (CONT'D)
          You're a pathetic loser. I wish you were
          dead!

Milly storms into her bedroom.

There are no new comments on the site as the Myth Mistress
sits down. Then one pops up.

INSERT: ROOMMATE TROUBLE? I CAN TAKE CARE OF THAT FOR YOU.

                    MYTH MISTRESS
          Who the hell are you?

INSERT: WHO DO YOU THINK?

                    MYTH MISTRESS (cont'd)
          Milly...

INSERT: IS MILLY A KILLER?

                    MYTH MISTRESS (cont'd)
          She's psycho enough...

Room view camera shows Milly, still dressed as Bo Peep,
sneaking out of her room. Myth Mistress doesn't notice her.

                    MYTH MISTRESS (cont'd)
          So, yeah, maybe.

Creeping slowly toward the Myth Mistress, she pulls out a
large knife.

Live comments pop onto the screen:

**INSERT: LOOK OUT! BEHIND YOU! BO PEEP IS ABOUT TO KILL
YOU!**

Myth Mistress sees Bo Peep/Milly on the live feed. She
turns.

Milly towers over her.

                    MILLY
          Toldja I'd kill you.

Myth Mistress looks at the clock.

CLOCK ON THE WALL READS 1 AM

Milly jabs wildly at her with the knife. Myth Mistress
dodges, ducks, and dives.

The fight is covered by all three camera angles.

> MYTH MISTRESS
> You're an hour late, you pathetic loon!

She kicks Milly in the face.

Milly lunges at her with the knife. Myth Mistress stops it
with her left hand. The knife goes through it.

> MILLY
> That's for calling me a loon, you rubber
> ho!

Myth Mistress kicks Milly in the stomach then removes the
knife from her own hand.

> MYTH MISTRESS
> Owww... shit that hurts! What the fuck
> is your problem, Milly?

> MILLY
> YOU! I told you that already, pinhead!

Milly rushes her, screaming like a maniac! She crashes into
Myth Mistress knocking them both to the ground.

The knife slides across the floor.

The full room view shows ANOTHER BO PEEP slowly creep out of
the bathroom.

The two combats continue without notice.

Milly kicks free and rushes to the knife. Picking it up, she
strolls slowly toward Myth Mistress.

> MYTH MISTRESS
> Milly, don't do this. What about grad
> school? Kill me and it'll hurt your
> chances of getting in.

> MILLY
> Grad school? You never listened to me.

Milly raises the knife above her head, rushing her...

> MILLY (cont'd)
> Die already, you phony skank!

... bringing the knife down hard.

Myth Mistress stops her arms with both hands, struggling to
keep the knife inches from her face.

> MYTH MISTRESS
> Milly stop... please, Milly... please...

An eerie eek emanates from Milly's body.

The two stunned women stop fighting and look at her chest.

Milly drops her knife. The point of a large blade pokes out
of her chest, creeping further and further through her.

                         MILLY
               Oww...
                    (grabbing it)
               Fuck...

Milly falls on the floor, staring at the Myth Mistress.

                         MILLY (cont'd)
                    (dying)
               I fucking hate you...

                         ANOTHER BO PEEP (O.S.)
               I told you there would be more killings
               before you were dead.

                         MYTH MISTRESS
               Why? What the fuck is going on? Who are
               you?

                         ANOTHER BO PEEP
               It had to look like a serial killer, so I
               could get away with it.

                         MYTH MISTRESS
               But so many people are watching. I have
               cameras everywhere. They know the whole
               story now.

                         ANOTHER BO PEEP
               Who cares. Oh, thanks for letting me
               kill Milly, by the way. I hated that
               bitch, too.

                         MYTH MISTRESS
               How do you know Milly? Or me, for that
               matter?

                         ANOTHER BO PEEP
               Who doesn't know the famously hot Myth
               Mistress and her sexy website?

Bo Peep strolls around waving the knife as she speaks.

                         ANOTHER BO PEEP (cont'd)
               As for Milly, well... let's just say we
               have history. Maybe she was the one that
               got away.

                    MYTH MISTRESS
You're lucky then.

                    ANOTHER BO PEEP
Ha! Not so much. You don't know
anything about Milly. She had
everything. I had nothing.

                    MYTH MISTRESS
Well, you're one up on her now, I'd say.

                    ANOTHER BO PEEP
Shut up, stupid! You don't know what she
put me through. Is was supposed to be
her, not me. I'm the sane one.

                    MYTH MISTRESS
I agree. Just put down the knife and
let's go have a cold one.

                    ANOTHER BO PEEP
Fuck you. You don't know me.

                    MYTH MISTRESS
But I want to... isn't that enough?

                    ANOTHER BO PEEP
Milly was right. You are a cocky bitch
with a smart ass mouth.

Bo Peep turns her head giving Myth Mistress the opening to
rush her. CRASH! She smashes Bo Peep's face into the wall
sending her mask flying.

Myth Mistress spins her around and sees a familiar face.

                    MYTH MISTRESS
Milly?!!

                    ANOTHER BO PEEP/MAGEE
No, you moron. I just killed Milly! I'm
Magee. Her twin sister. The sane one.
Didn't Milly ever talk about me?

                    MYTH MISTRESS
Well... we didn't exactly have the kind
of relationship where we share insane
twin sister stories.

                    ANOTHER BO PEEP/MAGEE
I was supposed to be here with her, not
you! We talked about going off to
college together all our lives before...

                    MYTH MISTRESS
          Before you went nuts, you mean?

Magee lunges in anger. Myth Mistress moves her upper body to
avoid the knife and knees Magee in the face.

Magee grabs her bleeding nose.

                    ANOTHER BO PEEP/MAGEE
          You made me bleed, you bitch. I'll kill
          you for that.

                    MYTH MISTRESS
          You were going to kill me anyway.

                    ANOTHER BO PEEP/MAGEE
          I'll make it hurt more than!

                    MYTH MISTRESS
          Why? What is your major malfunction, you
          batty knife-wielding lunatic?

                    ANOTHER BO PEEP/MAGEE
          Milly was the one mom and dad had
          committed. Not me! I'm sane. She
          tricked me into taking her place.

                    MYTH MISTRESS
          So, you're the genius of the family?

                    ANOTHER BO PEEP/MAGEE
          We're sisters. I felt sorry for her.
          She was sixteen and missed her boyfriend.
          It was only supposed to be one night
          while she fucked him for the first and
          last time. She was the evil one. She
          killed our parents and left me in there
          for over five years.

                    MYTH MISTRESS
          You're out now. Let's keep it that way.
          You let me go and I won't say anything to
          anybody.

                    ANOTHER BO PEEP/MAGEE
          Do you think I'm as dumb as Milly?

                    MYTH MISTRESS
          Well, she did trick you into taking her
          place in a mental institution.

                    ANOTHER BO PEEP/MAGEE
          You just told me you're live streaming
          over the internet. Everyone's seen my
          face now, too.

                    MYTH MISTRESS
          You still have your padded cell to go
          back to. Better than being dead, don't
          you think?

                    ANOTHER BO PEEP/MAGEE
          Who's gonna kill me, you? Ha! I don't
          think so. Five years in a place like
          that teaches you things.

Magee rushes her burying the knife deep into Myth Mistress'
stomach. She grabs it and knees Magee in the vagina.

Heavy footsteps move quickly down the hall toward the door.

                    MYTH MISTRESS
          They're coming for you. Better run while
          you can.

Magee grabs her by the hair yanking her around wildly.

                    ANOTHER BO PEEP/MAGEE
          I'm not going anywhere until you're dead!

Myth Mistress screams pulling the knife free...

                    MYTH MISTRESS
          Aaaaaaagggg!!!

...then stabbing Magee in the forehead with it.

                    ANOTHER BO PEEP/MAGEE
          Oww, you bitch...

Magee drops to the floor, motionless.

Two POLICE OFFICERS bust in, guns train on Myth Mistress.

                    POLICE OFFICER #1
          Drop the knife! Now!

                    MYTH MISTRESS
               (dropping the knife)
          Hey, it's not me. She's the killer.

The two officers rush her and throw her up against the wall.

                    POLICE OFFICER #2
               (cuffing her)
          Tell it to the girl with the knife in her
          face.

                    MYTH MISTRESS
          I'm telling the truth. This whole thing
          was broadcast over the internet. Check
          it out! It's all on my hard drive!

                    POLICE OFFICER #1
          We will. Don't worry.

The two officers cuff Magee who's barely coherent.

                    POLICE OFFICER #2
          Take sexy downstairs... I'll bring this
          one.

EXT. DORM - AMBULANCE - LATER

Myth Mistress is being worked on by an EMT. A comment pops
on her screen.

**INSERT: YOU THINK THIS IS OVER? BO PEEP IS GOING TO KILL
YOU STILL! WE WILL BE TOGETHER FOREVER... IN DEATH.**

Myth Mistress looks around. Milly is in a body bag, Magee
is in a moving ambulance.

                    MYTH MISTRESS
          OMG! I'm sick and tired of you psychos!
          Who are you fucker?

INSERT: I'M THE ONE FOR YOU. WE'RE MEANT FOR EACH OTHER.

                    MYTH MISTRESS (cont'd)
          Well, I'm pulling the plug on this night,
          Romeo! Ciao, people.

Myth Mistress turns off her phone.

BANG! Magee's ambulance crashes into a tree.

Myth Mistress runs to the ambulance.

Looking in the back, she sees Magee is gone. She rushes to
help the dazed driver, holding her bandaged stomach.

                    MYTH MISTRESS (cont'd)
          What happened?

                    AMBULANCE DRIVER
          Bo Peep...

                    MYTH MISTRESS
          Magee. I know. She's gone.

                    AMBULANCE DRIVER
          No. The one who did this... he was
          dressed like Bo Peep.

                    MYTH MISTRESS
          Another fucking Bo Peep?

                    AMBULANCE DRIVER
          There were fourteen killings tonight.
          Didn't you know that?

                    MYTH MISTRESS
               (scanning the area)
          Fourteen?! What the fuck?!
               (thinking)
          You know what that means?

                    AMBULANCE DRIVER
          A lot of dead students.

                    MYTH MISTRESS
          No! Well, yeah, but it also means
          Milly's psychic was right!

                    BO PEEP KILLER (O.S.)
          You're mine. That's why I killed anyone
          that got close to you. I want us to be
          together... forever link in our own
          folklore.

                    MYTH MISTRESS
               (looking around)
          Yeah, I know, I read all your post.

The Bo Peep Killer steps out from behind a large tree.

                    MYTH MISTRESS (cont'd)
          One question... before we die in each
          other's arms, etc.
               (beat)
          How do you even know me?

                    BO PEEP KILLER
          I've known you since your site went up.
          Your show inspired me.

                    MYTH MISTRESS
          I was worried something like this might
          happen.

                    BO PEEP KILLER
          What can I say, I always wanted to kill
          and tonight you gave me the perfect
          opportunity.

                    MYTH MISTRESS
          Yeah, I get it. It's classic pyscho...

                    BO PEEP KILLER
          Your internet fame becomes my internet
          fame... forever linked.

                    MYTH MISTRESS
          Listen, dude, you're nothing but a fucked
          in the head fan who's lost his shit and
          is trying to kill me. That's how you'll
          be remembered!

Her comments anger him.

                    BO PEEP KILLER
          Don't say that.

                    MYTH MISTRESS
          Why not? It's true.

                    BO PEEP KILLER
          It hurts!

                    MYTH MISTRESS
          So? You don't think killing me isn't
          going to hurt me, dumbass?! Fuck you!
               (she takes a deep breath)
          You know what... come here, lover. I'm
          ready...

They walk toward each other. He stops.

                    MYTH MISTRESS (cont'd)
          What's the matter pussy? Can't get it
          up? Lose your balls in a tragic jump
          rope incident in the third grade?
               (becoming dominate)
          I order you to come here right now and
          kiss me!

He steps toward her then stops.

                    MYTH MISTRESS (cont'd)
          NOW, LOSER! You're mine! I'm yours!
          Remember?

She reaches out to him. He moves closer. She kicks him in
the balls, dropping him to his knees.

                    MYTH MISTRESS (cont'd)
          Ah, so you do have balls.

As he's getting up, she punches him in the face hard!

He punches her even harder, staggering her.

Woozy from the punch, she moves away as fast as she can, knowing she's in serious jeopardy.

                    MYTH MISTRESS (cont'd)
          Shit...

He stalks her slowly, looking at his watch.

                    BO PEEP KILLER
          You bitch. It's time for you to die.

                    MYTH MISTRESS
               (running)
          Me, first? Why don't you go first? I'll
          follow.

                    BO PEEP KILLER
          I told you I'd kill you at midnight.

                    MYTH MISTRESS
          What time is it, anyway?

                    BO PEEP KILLER
          3 am. Midnight, Pacific time.

She stops.

                    MYTH MISTRESS
          OMG, you idiot! We're in the central
          time zone. It's 1 am Pacific!

                    BO PEEP KILLER
               (momentarily confused)
          Huh?

                    MYTH MISTRESS
          You chucklehead.

She kicks him in the balls, again. Dropping him to his knees. Again.

                    MYTH MISTRESS (cont'd)
          Do men just not believe a woman will kick
          them in the balls over and over or
          something?

As he stands up, he pulls out a large knife.

                    MYTH MISTRESS (cont'd)
          Damn! Does everyone carry a fucking huge
          butcher knife these days!

                         BO PEEP KILLER
          You shouldn't have done that.

                         MYTH MISTRESS
          You shouldn't be trying to kill me, dude!
          I think a kick in the nads is better than
          death! Okay, two kicks in the nads...

He moves at her quickly.

A shot rings out.

The bullet hits him in the back, knocking him on top of her,
and dropping them both to the ground.

                         MYTH MISTRESS (cont'd)
                    (struggling to breathe)
          I can't breathe. I can't breathe.

The two cops run up and yank the large dead man off her.

She's been stabbed twice, punched, kicked, and landed on.
She's cover with bandages and blood... but she's not beaten.

Moaning as she struggles to stand up, two more COPS put their
arms around her and help her to an ambulance.

                         MYTH MISTRESS (cont'd)
          He said he loved me...

                         COP ONE
          Oh, yeah?

                         MYTH MISTRESS
          Price of internet fame, huh, fellas?

                         COP
          You're lucky you're still alive.

                         MYTH MISTRESS
          Eh... I like to think of myself as kind
          of a badass... a smart sexy one.

They share a laugh as they sit her down on the back of the
ambulance. She turns on her iPhone.

Live comments are still streaming on the website. She begins
broadcasting.

                         MYTH MISTRESS (cont'd)
          This is Myth Mistress dot com, the
          internet's go-to source for total
          immersion into urban myths and legends.
          And boy, were we immersed tonight!
                    (beat)

                    MYTH MISTRESS (CONT'D)
          Here at Myth Mistress dot com, we don't
          deal in fact or fiction, our *raison
          d'etre* are things that go bump in the
          night... be they ghosts, demons, deranged
          fans on killing sprees, or a psycho-bitch
          roommate and her lunatic sister.
                    (thinking)
          Wait. No Milly was committed. Magee was
          just... unbalanced.
                    (beat)
          Ah, fuck them! They were both bat-shit
          crazy.
                    (beat)
          Well, I'm very happy to report that I
          made it... I'm still alive. I have one
          less fan `cause he got shot and fell on
          top of me. Sorry, you didn't get to see
          that... but you got to see most of it.

She looks at the viewer counter. It reads, 1,000,001

                    MYTH MISTRESS (cont'd)
                    (excited)
          All ONE MILLION of you! Excuse me, one
          million and one of you!

She smiles.

                    MYTH MISTRESS (cont'd)
          We all finally witnessed a first-hand
          account of an urban legend! Well, you
          got to see it. I lived it!
                    (beat)
          This was one hell of a Halloween. Can't
          wait for the next live stream event.
          Tell your friends!!

The EMT approaches her. She stands up.

                    MYTH MISTRESS (cont'd)
          Well, it's been real, and it's been fun,
          but I can't say it's been real fun.
                    (beat)
          Good night, everyone.

She turns off her phone ending the broadcast.

The EMT helps her up into the back of the ambulance.

                    MYTH MISTRESS (cont'd)
          Put me somewhere soft...

                         THE END

                                        FADE OUT.